THE KING
WITHOUT A HEART

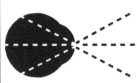

This Large Print Book carries the
Seal of Approval of N.A.V.H.

THE KING
WITHOUT A HEART

BARBARA CARTLAND

THORNDIKE PRESS

A part of Gale, a Cengage Company

Farmington Hills, Mich • San Francisco • New York • Waterville, Maine
Meriden, Conn • Mason, Ohio • Chicago

Copyright © 2008 by Cartland Promotions.
Thorndike Press, a part of Gale, a Cengage Company.

ALL RIGHTS RESERVED
The characters and situations in this book are entirely imaginary and bear no relation to any person or actual happening.
Thorndike Press® Large Print Gentle Romance.
The text of this Large Print edition is unabridged.
Other aspects of the book may vary from the original edition.
Set in 19 pt. Plantin.

LIBRARY OF CONGRESS CIP DATA ON FILE.
CATALOGUING IN PUBLICATION FOR THIS BOOK
IS AVAILABLE FROM THE LIBRARY OF CONGRESS

ISBN-13: 978-1-4328-4182-9 (hardcover)
ISBN-10: 1-4328-4182-3 (hardcover)

Published in 2017 by arrangement with Cartland Promotions

Printed in Mexico
1 2 3 4 5 6 7 21 20 19 18 17

"Everyone, but everyone can enjoy the rapture and joys of love, from the King himself to the lowest in the land."

Barbara Cartland

CHAPTER ONE:
1888

The Duke of Starbrooke finished the family prayers and the servants filed out of the dining room.

When they had gone the family moved to the table where breakfast was waiting for them and the butler and two footmen began to serve them.

As they did so the door opened and a young girl came nervously into the room.

She was small, slight and very pretty, but the expression on her face at the moment was one of anxiety.

She walked up to the Duke and bent to kiss his cheek.

"Why were you not at prayers, Titania?" he asked sharply.

"I am sorry, Uncle Edward, but I was delayed when I came back from riding."

"Delayed?" questioned the Duchess of Starbrooke from the end of the table. "That is only a word to cover up your carelessness in not noting the time."

"I am sorry, Aunt Louise," murmured Titania.

"So you should be," replied the Duchess. "If I have any more nonsense I shall tell your uncle to forbid you to ride each morning. It is a waste of time anyway."

Titania gave a gasp.

Yet as she sat down at the breakfast table, she knew it was her own fault.

It had been a lovely morning and as she had ridden through the woods that she loved, she had forgotten everything and for the moment she was feeling happy.

She reached a pool in the woods which was her favourite place, because she believed that the water nymphs lived there.

It was then that she realised that time was marching on and if she was late for prayers she would be in trouble.

She had ridden Mercury back as quickly as she could.

Even so, when she had changed her clothes and run downstairs the dining room door was closed.

She could hear her uncle's stentorian voice reading a prayer and those who had been listening to him intoned a respectful *amen.*

Then as the servants began to move out, she hurried in knowing that she was in trouble.

However, to her relief there was no long lecture, which she would normally have received on such occasions.

The Duke, in a surprisingly good humour, was looking down at his letters, which had been placed as usual beside his plate, after having been carefully sorted by his secretary.

Bills and requests for money were dealt with in the office and only the private letters were taken to the Duke. There was one which he had opened first and he was reading it with a faint smile on his hard lips.

From the end of the table the Duchess was watching him quizzically, but she was far too controlled to ask him the contents of the letter before he was ready to tell her.

Sitting opposite Titania on the Duke's right was her cousin Lady Sophie Brooke, who had just enjoyed a Season in London and undoubtedly had been one of the most important *debutantes* of the year.

The Duke had given a ball for her and was planning another a little later in the summer to take place here at Starbrooke Hall.

All the notable neighbours in the County would be invited and Titania was wondering if there was any chance of her being allowed to attend this ball.

She had not been taken to London when the first ball was held, the excuse being that she was still in mourning for her father and mother. This was not strictly true as the twelve months, which was considered the correct period for mourning, had been over for three weeks.

Titania had been sensible enough to face the truth that her uncle did not want her at the London ball!

It was not only because he was

ashamed of her mother, but because she was so much prettier than her cousin.

Titania was not in the least conceited, but she recognised that she closely resembled her mother and while the Starbrooke family had been excessively rude to her father, Lord Rupert Brooke, everyone else had spoken about his wife's beauty.

They understood exactly why Lord Rupert had fallen in love with her.

The Duke of Starbrooke was like his father.

The fifth Duke had been determined to keep the blood of the Starbrookes as blue as it had been for the last two hundred years and had arranged his son's marriage

with Princess Louise of Hughdel-
berg.

It was not a particularly important
Principality, but there was a distant
connection with Queen Victoria
and no one could say Princess Louise was not the perfect wife for the
next Duke.

Unfortunately the second son,
Lord Rupert Brooke upset his father's plans.

He had insisted on marrying a
commoner.

He had gone to Scotland for the
salmon fishing and was staying with
a distinguished friend, where he
always enjoyed a freedom he did
not have at home.

If he wanted to go riding, he rode,
without there being a fuss about it.

In the same way if he wanted to go fishing he would leave the castle and just walk down to the river.

He did not have to be accompanied by ghillies or anyone else unless he particularly asked for them.

As it happened, Lord Rupert liked to be alone, especially in Scotland, as he found it a tremendous relaxation after the pomp and ceremony observed in his own home. And indeed for that matter in most of the great ancestral houses in which he stayed as a visitor.

"You can do as you please, Rupert, whenever you stay with me," his friend had said.

Lord Rupert often thought it was the one holiday in the year when he could really enjoy himself.

His friend, the Chieftain of a famous Clan, was fey because he was a Scot. He could understand people's inner feelings far better than any Englishman could possibly do.

This year, when Lord Rupert had come to stay, there were no other guests in the castle and he and the Laird spent the evenings discussing the issues that interested them both and it was what they had always done when they were at Oxford together.

Next morning Lord Rupert went down to the salmon river alone. He was carrying his own rod and a landing-net in which, when he had hooked and played his fish, he would take it from the river.

He had caught two salmon, when to his astonishment he hooked a really big fish.

It was bigger than any salmon he had ever seen in the river and he was determined not to lose it. He played it firmly but not roughly, knowing that because it was so heavy he must be careful not to snap his line.

The fish had come straight from the sea and fought like a tiger to regain its freedom.

It was a fearsome battle which Lord Rupert relished and he was equally determined to take home this great fish as a trophy for which he would certainly be congratulated.

The huge fish jumped and jumped again and as Lord Rupert let out his line, he was beginning to fear that the fish would get away.

He needed to find a way to lift it out of the water as the net he had brought with him was far too small and he had very stupidly left his gaff on the bank.

It was then to his relief, he realised that he had attracted an audience.

Coming down a path which led to the part of the river where he was standing was a young woman. He was not able to look at her, although one glance told him that she was present.

Instead he raised his voice,

"Can you help me, please?"

"Yes of course," the young woman answered.

"You will find my gaff on the bank."

"Yes, I can see it."

Now he had secured some help, it was only a question of a few minutes before he could bring the salmon in.

The girl gaffed it and then handed the fish to him to lift out of the river as it was far too heavy for her.

It was an extremely large salmon and would, Lord Rupert thought, weigh over twenty pounds and he was certain that his host would be delighted, as it was unusual to find such a large fish in this part of the river.

Then he looked at the girl who

had helped him and was astonished.

Smiling at him, because he had been so successful, was the most beautiful young woman he had ever seen.

She had a beauty that was different from any of the many lovely women whom Lord Rupert had associated with in London.

Because he was so handsome and the son of a Duke, he was invited to every party and every ball as well as to every alluring candlelit dinner given in Mayfair.

But of all the women he had pursued and who had pursued him, he had never seen anyone quite so lovely as the girl he was looking at now.

It was difficult for him to explain her difference from the others.

Her heart-shaped face was very young and innocent.

There was nothing flirtatious or provocative in the way she was looking at him with her large grey eyes, which seemed to fill her whole face and there was something magical about them.

In the same way she seemed to belong to the river and the moors rather than to the world in which he lived.

She was simply and correctly dressed, but Lord Rupert could see that her hair under her bonnet had touches of red that proclaimed to him her Scottish ancestry.

Yet he had never seen a Scot who

looked like her and he wondered if she was real.

It was later when he came to know her that he believed she was in fact part of a dream that had always been in his heart, but he thought it was something he would never find.

As Lord Rupert looked at Iona, Iona looked at him.

Something passed between them that was beyond words and was indeed inexplicable.

Quite simply they fell in love at first sight.

There was no question of Lord Rupert thinking again, as his father had begged him to do, nor would he postpone the date of their marriage.

He and Iona had found each other and nothing else in the world mattered.

Lord Rupert's father, the Duke, was furious, although he admitted that Iona was a lady and her father a respectable Chieftain of a small clan.

"But that," he shouted furiously to his son, "is not good enough for the Starbrookes."

It was doubtful if Lord Rupert listened or understood what was being said to him, as he was head over heels in love and merely counting the days until he could marry Iona.

He paid his own family the compliment of taking her to Starbrooke Hall with her parents before the wedding actually took place.

Because he behaved like a gentle-man, the Duke was polite to Iona's father and mother, but when he had his son alone, he raged at him.

"All right she is beautiful, I am not arguing about that," the Duke had thundered. "But all down the centuries the Brookes have married their equals and nothing you can say can make this woman our equal."

When Iona and her parents re-turned to Scotland, Lord Rupert travelled with them and they were married quietly by the Minister of the Kirk where Iona had been christened.

When they left on their honey-moon, Lord Rupert took his wife first to Paris and then on to Venice, Athens and Cairo. He wanted her to see the world and he hoped it would amuse her as much as it had always fascinated and interested him.

She loved every moment of their honeymoon and everything they experienced, just in the same way that she loved him.

They were so perfectly attuned to each other that they never had to explain to the other what they were thinking or what they wanted as they each knew instinctively.

When Titania was born, both Lord Rupert and his wife adored their small daughter and it did not worry him that it would be very difficult for Iona to have any more children.

Her home was a home of love and joy because her parents were so supremely and completely happy and they both cherished their only child.

Titania travelled with them, sleeping in many strange places. Sometimes in a tent or on the back or a camel.

Occasionally she cuddled up between her father and mother in the open air, when they were exploring unknown territory and could find nowhere else to sleep at night.

It was an education which most boys would have enjoyed, but most girls would have found uncomfortable.

Titania enjoyed every moment of

it and for her the whole world consisting of her father and mother was one of love.

Then tragically Lord Rupert and his wife were killed in a railway crash when they were travelling home after a short visit to Wales.

For Titania it was the end of the first part of her life.

Overnight as it were, she ceased to be a child, because her parents were no longer alive and she became a woman with all the difficulties and troubles that lie in wait for those who have been forced to grow up too quickly.

When the funeral was over, Titania's uncle ordered her to pack her boxes.

"You are coming to live with me

at Starbrooke Hall," he commanded.

She tried to persuade him to allow her to remain in the house where she had been born. She had been so happy there with her father and mother, but he had told her curtly it was impossible.

She was informed later that the house was to be sold with all its contents and she was not permitted to keep even some small pieces of furniture that she particularly loved.

Only with Nanny's help was she able to save some small ornaments, which her mother had always prized and Titania kept them hidden from her uncle.

In fact there were only two things

the Duke allowed her to take with her to Starbrooke Hall.

One was Nanny who had looked after her since she was a baby and the Duke had said somewhat grudgingly she could be Titania's lady's maid.

The second was her horse Mercury, which her father had given her the year before and which now she loved more than anyone else in the whole world.

She told all her troubles to Mercury and he seemed to understand and it was Mercury who made life worth living because she could ride him every morning.

The reason she was so unhappy at Starbrooke Hall was, to put it mildly, mental cruelty.

Her father and mother were dead, but the people around her were continually in one way or another pointing out how wrong it had been for her father to make such an inferior marriage.

And then of course to produce her.

It was not what they said in words.

It was the way they looked and the tone of her aunt's voice when she spoke to her.

Lady Sophie was a year older than Titania and she soon discovered how clever her cousin was at arranging hair and how beautifully she sewed.

After that Titania became more or less an unpaid lady's maid.

It was — "Titania, do my hair — Titania, mend this lace — Titania, fetch my bag."

Titania was much quicker and much more effective than anyone who had looked after Sophie before and she was therefore in demand almost every hour of the day.

The only time she could escape was very early in the morning and as her cousin slept late she could go riding alone on Mercury.

Because her uncle considered her of no importance, she did not have to be accompanied by a groom.

Titania often found it difficult to fulfil all Sophie's demands, but at the same time she had her moments of happiness.

Apart from riding Mercury she

had discovered the library at the Hall and found all the books her father had prized so much, but which she had not been allowed to keep when their house was sold.

There were also a great many others which she knew he had read when he was a young man and he had often quoted them to her when they were having one of their exciting and interesting discussions.

Just as he had talked to his Scottish friend and then to Iona, Lord Rupert had talked to his daughter.

He taught her far more than any governess could have done and the books that she had studied in her father's library and now in her uncle's completed her education.

Lord Rupert had learnt a great

number of languages because he loved travelling around the world.

It amused him when Titania was small to speak to her in French and make her try to pronounce the words after he had said them.

The same applied to other languages and when she grew older she found that a number of books in her father's library were in a variety of languages. As she was intelligent she forced herself to understand them, just as her mother had done when she found where her husband's interests lay and was determined to share them.

Another factor she had found almost intolerable at Starbrooke Hall was that neither the Duchess nor her daughter ever talked about anything except the latest gossip or what the newspapers were reporting about the social entertainments in London.

Titania often thought that if she could not go to bed to read one of the books from the library, she would have wanted to scream at the boredom of it all.

None of the family had the slightest idea that she was reading books that her father would have enjoyed, but which would have been considered completely and absolutely incomprehensible to any other young woman.

Equally it was a very lonely life.

There was only Mercury to hear which exciting incidents in history she had discovered the night before or a poem she had found written by an ancient Greek, which was ringing in her ears so that she must recite it to him.

Now as she finished her breakfast, Titania was thinking that she had been unexpectedly fortunate in not being scolded very angrily for being late for prayers, although her aunt's words had scalded her.

Her uncle usually considered lateness to be an unforgivable sin.

However this morning having reproved her, he was reading a letter which lay on top of his pile and apparently had no more to say to her.

She was just contemplating whether she could slip away from

the table without being noticed when the Duke announced,

"I have something to tell you all, which I think will surprise and at the same time please you."

"It sounds most intriguing," muttered the Duchess.

She glanced at her daughter Sophie as she spoke and Sophie, who had been thinking of something else, immediately turned her head towards her father.

Titania realised it would be impossible for her to leave the room and therefore sat waiting expectantly for what the Duke had to say.

"I have received," he began, as he put his glasses on again, "a letter from Velidos, which I am sure you will all find extremely interesting."

Thinking quickly Titania remembered that a month ago the Crown Prince Frederick of Velidos had come to stay after a visit to London, where apparently he had met her uncle and aunt and Sophie.

She had thought him a rather plain, dull young man and there had been something else about him which she had not liked.

She could not explain exactly what it was, but she had her mother's gift of being fey and was seldom wrong when she summed up a man or woman with whom she came into contact.

She had not been particularly interested in Prince Frederick and therefore apart from curtsying to him she had not had any close contact with him.

"Of course we all remember the Crown Prince," commented the Duchess. "A charming young man and with the good manners that so many Englishmen lack."

It was the sort of remark she often made when she compared the English to the men of her own country who were always spoken about as if they had every talent under the sun.

"I have here a letter from the Crown Prince," the Duke was saying somewhat pompously, "in which he asks that Sophie shall proceed as soon as possible to Velidos, where to his great delight his brother, the King, has given permission for their marriage."

The Duchess gave a little exclamation of delight, but Titania was completely astonished.

She had no idea or else she had not listened very carefully that the Crown Prince wished to marry Sophie or that it had been arranged by her uncle.

He was quite obviously delighted at the idea of his daughter being united with a Royal family, even though it was not at all an important one. Because the bridegroom was a Crown Prince there was obviously some likelihood that he would later become King.

The Duke was waiting for his daughter's response to his announcement and Sophie simpered demurely,

"I am delighted at the news, Papa.

How soon will we be leaving for Velidos?"

"*You* will be leaving, my dear," replied the Duke. "Your future husband has of course invited your mother and me to accompany you, but I am afraid it is impossible for me to get away immediately, which is what he requires, because of my duties at Windsor Castle."

Titania was aware that the Duke's attendance at Windsor Castle was something he looked forward to and nothing or no one could prevent him from being there.

From what she gathered his duties were hereditary and not very arduous and he had no intention of trying to change them or failing to do what was expected of him.

"If you are not coming with me," said Sophie plaintively, "it will be very frightening going to a strange country when I cannot even speak the language."

"I said I cannot go," added the Duke testily, "but your mother will of course accompany you and your future husband says in this letter that a member of the Cabinet will be in attendance on you as well as two Ladies-in-Waiting, a gentleman usher and several other members of the Royal Household."

"Well that will be all right, I suppose, but I shall miss you, Papa."

"And I shall miss you, my dear, and I regret not attending your wedding, but as soon as possible you must bring your husband to stay with us here, perhaps for the shooting or hunting in the autumn."

Sophie looked pleased at this suggestion and then unexpectedly, she looked across the table.

"And I shall take Titania with me," she asserted haughtily. "No one else can do my hair as well as she can."

"But I cannot go," Titania exclaimed quickly without thinking.

"Why ever not," Sophie asked aggressively.

"I would have to leave Mercury behind and I am sure there will be excellent hairdressers in Velidos."

"I have never heard such nonsense," intervened the Duchess sharply. "If your cousin wants you to accompany her, Titania, you will go and think yourself extremely lucky. Most girls of your age would be delighted to travel abroad."

She rose from the table as she spoke and Titania recognised that it was no use arguing.

However her heart sank as if she once left England and Mercury and Nanny, which were all that remained of her life, what would happen to her in the future?

Almost as if the Duke was reading her mind he said,

"You will go with your cousin, Titania, and, as your aunt says, you should think yourself a very fortunate girl. When Sophie has settled down perhaps in six months or a year, you will come back and I shall find a suitable husband for you."

He paused for a moment before continuing,

"Unfortunately not someone very grand, seeing what a bad marriage your father made, but at least you have the advantage of being my niece and that should count for a great deal."

Titania drew in her breath.

She had always been afraid that this was what her uncle would say to her one day.

She had known, when he had been busy arranging Sophie's marriage, he was determined it would be with someone grand and then that he would eventually come round to arranging hers.

She had no intention of marrying

someone chosen for her by her uncle and someone she did not love.

She could remember her father saying over and over again,

"I am the luckiest man alive, Titania, because I married your mother who I love so deeply and who loves me. I was not pushed up the aisle with some stupid woman who wanted my title or whose family considered themselves the equal of mine."

He had laughed when he finished speaking and then added,

"Your mother to me is the Queen of Love and the Princess of Happiness. What man could ask for a finer pedigree than that?"

Titania had smiled at him and

became determined that when she married she would be as happy as her father and mother were together.

If ever her father had been away for the day, her mother would wait for his return and when she heard him come in at the front door, she would then run towards him, put her arms round his neck and pull his head down to hers.

"You are — home! Oh, darling, how — much I have — missed you."

Titania could now hear her voice saying those very words.

"As I have missed you, my precious one," her father would reply.

Then he would kiss her mother and it would be some time before he would stop kissing her.

That was love!

That was what living meant with someone you adored and who adored you.

It was what Titania wanted to find, even if she remained unmarried until she died, but she knew it was no use explaining her feelings to her uncle.

She must wait until her bridegroom had been chosen for her and then she would have to be brave enough to insist that she would not marry him.

She could imagine only too well how furious her uncle would be and how disagreeable her aunt.

That, however, was not the problem at the moment.

As if her father was prompting her, Titania knew she must accompany Sophie, even though it meant leaving Mercury behind.

She did not say any more, but followed her aunt and Sophie from the dining room. Only when they were outside and walking towards the hall did Titania slip away.

She ran down the passage and up the secondary staircase which led up to the first floor and there was another flight up to the second. She was running so quickly that she was almost breathless when she reached the top.

She opened the door of the sewing room where she knew she would find Nanny.

She was an elderly woman who

had come to Lady Rupert when Titania was born. She had loved the small baby who had been placed in her arms and she had given Titania her whole devotion over the years.

For one terrifying moment, after her mother and father had died, Titania was afraid that her uncle would not allow Nanny to accompany her to Starbrooke Hall.

"Nanny will not only look after me," she had told him, "but help the seamstress if you have one. She is wonderful with a needle and Mama always said there was no one like her."

It was fortunate that at that moment the Starbrooke seamstress was growing old and the Duchess was already talking of having to look for a new one.

So Nanny had gone with Titania and she made the parting from her home a little easier to bear than it might have been.

Now she opened the door of the sewing room to find Nanny, as she expected, sitting by the window mending a pillowcase.

She ran across the room towards her and before Nanny could even move, Titania flung her arms around her neck.

"Oh, Nanny! Nanny!" she cried, *"I cannot bear it."*

"What is it, dearie?" asked Nanny. "What can have upset you so?"

"Sophie is to marry the — Crown Prince of Velidos," sobbed Titania, "and I have to go with her — just because I can do her hair."

Nanny did not say anything, she only held Titania tightly.

"How can I go away and leave — Mercury?" wept Titania, "and how can I leave — you? Uncle Edward says I can come — back when Sophie is settled, but only because he — intends to find a — husband for me. Oh, Nanny, I cannot bear it."

"Perhaps it won't be as bad as you expect, dearie," Nanny soothed her. "And it will be a change for you to travel abroad as you used to do with your father and mother and loved every moment of it."

"But that was because — I was with them and — not with Sophie."

"Well you never know there might

be interesting things to see and I'll remind His Grace that he said you could come home when her Ladyship's settled down."

Titania wiped away her tears.

"I suppose you will think — I am not being sensible, Nanny, but I have — lost Papa and Mama — and the house where I was so happy, and now I have to — lose you and — Mercury and there is nothing left — *nothing*."

"Now what I'll do," said Nanny sensibly, "is make you a nice cup of tea. You'll feel better after that."

"No thank you. I have just had breakfast. It's not tea I want, Nanny, but to — go back to our — little house — where we were all — so happy."

"You can't put back the clock, dearie, that is something you can't ever do in life. But going to that place where her Ladyship's getting married will be something new and might even be exciting."

"I doubt it," sniffled Titania. "Papa used to laugh at those small Balkan countries and say they were all much of a muchness and he would much rather climb the — Himalayas or walk across the — African desert."

"That sounds very like your father and from what I hear of the African desert it's too hot and too dry and you have to go for miles and miles to find a drink of water."

Titania laughed as Nanny meant her to.

"Oh, Nanny, you always see the bright side of everything! If I don't have you to talk to and — of course Mercury who never answers back, I will be so miserable and will — cry myself to sleep — every night."

"That'll be very silly," Nanny scolded her, "making yourself look plain and spoiling your eyes. You listen to me. When you get to this place you'll find something to amuse you and, who knows, perhaps it's your father — God bless his soul — taking you away from this mountain of misery."

Titania laughed again and it was a very pretty sound.

"Oh, Nanny, darling Nanny, you always cheer me up and of course you are quite right. It will be a change to get away from here and not have to listen to everyone telling me over and over again what a mistake it was for Papa to have married Mama."

"She was indeed a gift from God Himself," Nanny told her, "and that's what your father always believed her to be. I've never in all my life known a man so happy and just you remember that when they say anything to you."

"It's not exactly what they say," answered Titania. "It's the way they look and the note in their voices and they speak to me as if I was something out of the gutter that had crawled in by mistake."

Nanny gave her a little shake.

"Now you're not to talk like that.

I taught you when you were small to see the bright side of life and the best side of people. If they're unpleasant and disagreeable, it's hurting them more than it's hurting you. Always remember that."

"Oh, Nanny, I love you so much. If I do have to go away, you must write to me every day and tell me how Mercury is and make me laugh by the things you say otherwise I shall just sit — crying until I come home."

"You'll do nothing of the sort. That would make your father very angry."

Titania thought for a moment and then she said,

"You are quite right, Nanny, he would be ashamed of me running away from an adventure! That is what this has to be. If I have to stay there any longer than six months, I will go on my knees to the King and ask him to let you come out and join me."

"That'll be the day," muttered Nanny.

She took out her clean handkerchief and wiped Titania's eyes and then glanced at the clock.

"If you ask me," she said, "her Ladyship'll be wanting you to do something for her and making a fuss if you don't turn up."

"Yes, Nanny," agreed Titania with a little sigh. "I had better go down and see what is wanted. I understand now why we had to shop and shop when we were in London. I could not think why she wanted all those clothes."

"They'll be her trousseau. I don't have to guess far that I'll be sewing a whole lot of them one way or the other before you go."

Titania kissed Nanny on both cheeks.

"I love you Nanny. You always make me laugh when I want to cry."

"As I've told you often enough before, dearie, no woman looks her best with swollen eyes. And crying never got you anywhere, that's for sure."

Titania kissed her again.

"I am going down smiling," she resolved, "and telling myself, although it is a lie, that I want to go to Velidos."

She ran from the room as she was speaking.

Nanny gave a deep sigh and sat down again.

She knew better than Titania knew herself how much the girl was suffering. It was bad enough to lose her father and mother and the home where she had been so happy.

It was worse still to be in a place where she was not wanted.

There was no love here. Only a pompous appreciation of blue blood and an exaggerated idea of their own importance.

'After all,' Nanny said to herself, 'with all this hoity-toity from His Grace, whatever the colour of their blood they all of them bleeds when someone pricks them!'

Then she picked up her sewing and carried on with her work.

CHAPTER TWO

During the next few days there was pandemonium at Starbrooke Hall.

Sophie flew into a temper because she was not as pleased with her trousseau as she thought she would be and insisted on going to London for another fitting for her wedding dress.

This was a relief to Titania because she could ride as much as she wished and there was no one to find some task for her every minute of the day.

However her apprehension at having to leave for Velidos grew and grew. It was one thing to go abroad with her father and mother which she had loved and quite another to be travelling with Sophie who treated her merely as a servant.

She learned from the Duchess that Sophie was to be allocated two Ladies-in-Waiting from Velidos and she was to be the third and obviously inferior to the other two.

"What can I do?" she asked Nanny pitifully. "How can I go where there will be no one I can talk to and no one who will be interested in me as a person?"

"I expect you'll find that quite a lot of people will be," Nanny soothed her. "You know how your parents always made friends in those strange countries where no Englishman had been seen before."

She paused for a moment and then she added,

"I know what you must do, dearie, and this is the truth, you must be able to talk the language before you get there."

Titania's eyes lit up.

"Oh, Nanny," she exclaimed, "you are so clever! I was thinking I would pick up the language quite easily when I reached Velidos. But if I can speak it before I arrive, that of course would be a great help to me."

"It shouldn't be difficult for you, seeing as how many foreigners you've spoken to one way or another. Your father always said that you were as good as he was when it came to making yourself understood in a strange place."

"Now you are flattering me, but, of course, I am so unhappy at leaving you and Mercury."

"Perhaps something will happen which'll bring you back. You've just got to trust God to look after you or, if it comes to that, your father and mother. Wherever they be, they'll be thinking of you and praying for you."

"Of course they will," agreed Titania. "And when I'm in trouble, I will talk to Papa and ask him to guide me as he did when he was alive."

"You do just that and you'll find

everything will come right one way or another."

Nanny sounded most optimistic to Titania, but when she was alone she became worried. She knew how unpleasant the Duke and Duchess had been to the girl and in her opinion Lady Sophie treated her as if she came from the gutter.

There was, however, nothing Nanny could do and she promised Titania over and over again she would write to her and tell her about Mercury.

Whilst Sophie was in London Titania rode every hour of the day she could, but when her cousin arrived back no one talked about anything except clothes and as Nanny had predicted, a dozen garments needed to be altered at the last minute.

The Duke had spoken to Queen Victoria and Her Majesty had graciously ordered that Sophie and the wedding party, which included the Duchess, should travel to Velidos in a Battleship.

Titania had so often discussed the complex political situation in the Balkans with her father and she therefore guessed secretly that the Queen was seizing on a good excuse to display the strength of Great Britain.

After Nanny's prompting Titania found her way to the library and read as much as she could about Velidos.

The country was situated on the

Aegean Sea a little north of Greece and this meant their language would contain many Greek words.

It made it easier for her that she also knew a smattering of several Balkan languages, as she had visited so many different countries with her father and mother.

There was of course nothing as helpful as a dictionary of the language of Velidos in the library and Titania wondered if it would be possible to find anyone in England who spoke the language.

She therefore suggested to Sophie that it would help her to engage a tutor.

"He could teach us," she proposed, "just the fundamental words of the language."

"Why should I bother about their stupid language?" demanded Sophie scornfully. "Frederick speaks very good English and he told me that most of the people in the Palace can do the same."

"But you will want to talk to the people in the towns," argued Titania, "and the countryside."

"If they cannot talk English," replied Sophie, "then they need not talk to me. That is what it amounts to."

Titania said no more.

She merely carried on trying to find more references to Velidos in the library, which was very difficult and since there was no one to ask what was available, she found it impossible to make much progress in such a short time.

The Duke had arranged his daughter's marriage with the approval of Queen Victoria and King Alexius of Velidos.

The King appreciated that the Duke was in a hurry for his daughter to be married and settled down in the country to which she would then belong.

The Crown Prince seemed to be equally as impatient and he wrote saying everything had been arranged.

The two Ladies-in-Waiting who were to accompany Lady Sophie would arrive in England on the 10th of May and be prepared to leave the next day in the British Battleship.

The Duchess protested it was impossible for them all to be ready in such a hurry, but the Duke paid no attention to her and this merely meant that Titania and Nanny had more to do.

Everyone in Starbrooke Hall seemed to be extremely sharp-tempered and Sophie kept complaining that she did not have enough clothes, her hats were not decorated enough and she could not possibly be ready to sail on the 11th of May.

No one paid any heed to what she was saying and the only person who had to listen was Titania.

There was no one to worry whether Titania had the right clothes except Nanny and it was she who finally insisted that they should send to London for several gowns. Titania bought them from the shop her mother had patronised when she was alive.

When she had come to live with her uncle at Starbrooke Hall, he had taken over her finances.

Her father had left her all he owned in his will and there was also the money that the Duke had received for her home when he sold it.

It was all in the bank but Titania was not allowed to spend it and she could not write a cheque without her uncle's permission.

She went to his study with the bills for the gowns, which Nanny had insisted on her taking with her and her uncle had looked at them critically and said he considered it was a tremendous waste of money.

"I should have thought your nurse could have made a dress for you," he remarked sharply.

"Nanny has always made the ordinary dresses I wear every day," answered Titania, "and of course my petticoats and blouses. But she thought I ought to take some gowns for an important occasion which I might have to attend with Sophie."

"I imagine that is most unlikely," said the Duke coldly, "although of course one never knows how foreigners will behave."

He spoke to her scornfully and it was with difficulty that Titania stopped herself from saying that her father had many friends who were foreigners.

She fervently hoped that she would make some friends in Velidos and she recognised that her uncle was determined to make her keep to the lowly position he had consigned her to because of her inferior breeding.

Grudgingly the Duke initialled the bills that Titania had presented him with and this meant they would be paid by his secretary.

Then Titania said,

"I shall, Uncle Edward, need some ready money if I am going to Velidos."

"Whatever for?" asked the Duke.

"I may have to buy some necessities there, I may have to tip some of the servants and I might wish to give a present to people who are kind to me."

"I should have thought that was quite unnecessary," exclaimed the Duke sternly. "How much do you require?"

Titania thought for a moment.

"I would like to have a thousand pounds paid into a bank account in Velidos. Or if you think that is too much then at least five hundred pounds."

The Duke thumped his clenched fist down on the desk.

"I have never known such non-sense!" he fumed. "No woman of your age should want so much money to spend on trinkets. You will be fed and housed and it is quite unnecessary for you to spend money that should be kept as a nest egg for your old age."

Titania drew in her breath before responding very quietly,

"It is *my* money, Uncle Edward, and I absolutely refuse to go to Velidos without a penny to my name and have to beg from strangers if I require anything that I have not brought with me."

Her uncle glared at her.

"You may think it is your money because your father left it to you, but who gave it to your father in the first place? I did, because I am Head of the family, and you know, or you should know, that in aristocratic families like ours the Head holds the purse-strings and allows what he thinks right to those members of his family he looks after."

Titania realised this to be true.

She had often thought her uncle was very unfair when he came into the title to make a smaller allowance to her father than he had formerly received from his own father.

Lord Rupert however had just shrugged his shoulders and said,

"My brother, Edward, has always been cheese-paring ever since he was a small boy. I am only astonished that he allows me anything and I am certainly not going to go down on my knees to ask for more."

He had not been short of money even with the Duke's meanness, as Titania's mother had fortunately been left quite a considerable sum by her godmother.

Her father had not been a rich man, although by Scottish standards he was well off.

Titania wondered now whether she should get in touch with her Scottish relations — perhaps they would have her to stay with them and save her from going to Velidos, but then she recognised that there would be a furious row if she ever suggested such an idea.

Instead she pleaded quietly,

"Please, Uncle Edward, let me have five hundred pounds to put into a bank in Velidos. I promise that I will spend as little as possible. I just want to feel safe in a foreign country."

Grumbling beneath his breath, the Duke finally agreed and when Titania left him, she knew she had been fortunate in winning the battle.

It was Nanny who packed her trunks and put in a lot of items she thought she might need that she would never have thought of herself.

Nanny had also made her two very pretty day dresses and promised to send her several others when she had finished them.

"I want you to look smart among all those strange people. Your mother always used to say that foreigners thought the English were dowdy and that's something you must not be."

"I remember Mama saying that," replied Titania, "and of course she was right. They do look dowdy abroad compared with the French who are so smart, while the Italians are always very glamorous in the evening."

"Well, you're going to be glamorous with what we've bought you," smiled Nanny, "and you hold your head high, dearie, and don't let anyone put on you. You're as good as they are, if not a lot better, and that goes for Lady Sophie for all her airs and graces."

Titania laughed because she could not help it. She knew that Nanny disliked Sophie in the same way as she disliked the Duchess.

"I do wish you were coming with

me, Nanny. At least we could have a good laugh at some of the things that will occur. As it is, I will have to keep a straight face. But I will write and tell you everything that happens to me."

"You do that, dearie, and as I'll be writing to you, we'll feel close to each other and that's the truth."

It was, however, very hard for Titania not to cry when she had to finally say goodbye to Mercury and then to Nanny.

"Promise me, Nanny," she implored her, "you will go and see Mercury every day. I know he will miss me and you must explain to him that I will come back as soon as I can, just to be with him."

"I'll try and make him understand

and don't you worry about him, just worry about yourself and have a good time, while her Ladyship will be giving herself airs as a Princess."

"What I have to find, Nanny, is someone who will laugh with me and not take anything that happens too seriously."

At the same time it was still agony to kiss Nanny goodbye and have her last quick hug with Mercury.

Then she climbed into the carriage which was to take them to London and there they would board the Battleship which was waiting to convey the bridal party to Velidos.

The Duchess made it very clear to Titania that despite the fact that she was her niece she was of no importance and she was therefore to keep in the background.

When the Duchess and Sophie swept aboard, the Captain of *H.M.S. Victorious* was waiting for them, while Titania was left to follow with her aunt's lady's-maid and a footman carrying the hand-luggage.

They were received on board first by the Captain and then by a Minister of State for Velidos, who had been sent to escort them together with the two Ladies-in-Waiting and an Equerry.

Titania saw at a glance that the Ladies-in-Waiting were elderly, plain and definitely pompous. She guessed they had been chosen because they could instruct Sophie on the importance of her position as wife of the Crown Prince and they would also explain her part in the marriage ceremony.

The Equerry was a young man who looked almost Greek and he had, Titania thought, a twinkle in his eye.

There was, however, no chance of anyone speaking except Sophie who was showing off and the Duchess was already complaining about the difficulties of travelling in a ship of war.

As it happened, Titania had been aboard quite a number of Battleships at one time or another, as her father had often called on Naval Captains in foreign ports where it was unusual to see an Englishman.

She thought as soon as her aunt and Sophie were settled into their cabins she might have a chance to explore the ship. However, she kept in the background, as she had been told to do.

It was only when they were underway and she went out on deck that the Equerry came and spoke to her.

"Are you looking forward to the voyage, Miss Brooke?"

"I love being at sea," she replied, "and I am thankful to say I am never seasick."

"If that is true, then this will certainly be an unusual voyage. I have never passed through the Bay of Biscay without every woman on board locking herself in her cabin."

Titania laughed.

"I can assure you I will not do that."

He was speaking quite good English and as he seemed friendly, Titania asked him,

"I wonder if you would do me a great favour."

"Of course I will do anything I can."

"I want to learn the language of your country," Titania told him, "and I do not think it will be difficult because I already speak Greek and a little of some of the other Balkan languages."

The Equerry looked at her in surprise.

"I have been told to teach a little of our language to Lady Sophie if possible, but I had no idea there would be anyone aboard who could speak Greek."

"As I have never heard anyone speak Velidosian, please say something to me in your language."

The Equerry gabbled off several sentences.

Titania said that she recognised several words amongst them.

"Now what did you say?" she asked.

"I said, 'you are so very pretty, Miss Brooke, and that you might have just arrived from Olympus and undoubtedly the Gods you have left behind will miss you.' "

Titania laughed.

"No wonder I found it difficult to guess what you were saying. Thank you for the compliment, but as unfortunately we are not going to Olympus, I want to learn as much Velidosian as I can."

"Very well," the Equerry replied. "Shall we set a time for your lessons?"

"Of course, and I suggest, if it suits you, eleven o'clock in the morning however rough the sea may be."

She knew as she spoke that the Equerry was quite certain she would not turn up while they were crossing the Bay of Biscay and she was also hoping that Sophie would not require her at that time.

When she entered Sophie's cabin to see if she had everything she wanted, her cousin asked sharply,

"Where have you been, Titania, and why are you not looking after me?"

"I am sorry. I was watching the ship move out of dock."

"Well, as Mama insists on Martha unpacking her trunks first, you can start on mine until Martha is free."

Titania, without making any comment, began to unpack Sophie's dressing case. She did, however, think to herself that her cousin might have said 'please.'

She never said 'thank you' for anything that was done for her.

"If there is one thing I hate," Sophie was saying, "it is being at sea. I know I am going to be seasick and the sooner I can lie down the better."

Although Titania said it was likely that the English Channel would be calm, Sophie insisted on getting into bed.

"I intend to stay here," she announced arrogantly, "until we arrive and it is no use arguing with me. What is more I have no wish to talk to those ugly old women who have been sent to accompany me."

"They are your Ladies-in-Waiting," cautioned Titania, "and they will take umbrage if you refuse to speak to them."

"Let them. Once I am married to Frederick, they will have to do as I tell them. After all as Crown Prince he is very, very important in Velidos."

"What about the King?" asked Titania.

She thought as she put the question there had been very little said about him. She knew, of course, that his name was Alexius and he was the elder brother of Prince Frederick who was marrying Sophie.

But neither her uncle nor her aunt had had anything to say about him, which seemed a little strange.

Then she told herself that the person who would be able to answer her questions was the Equerry. He, at least, seemed friendly.

Unless somebody prevented her from having lessons with him, she would be able to ask him everything she wanted to know.

The Captain's cabin had been put at Sophie's disposal and it was where they dined that evening.

The English Channel through which the ship was now moving was, Titania thought, as smooth as the proverbial duckpond. However, the Duchess said she preferred to eat in her own cabin and Sophie was already in bed.

The dinner party therefore consisted of the Captain, the Minister of State, who Titania found was a rather charming man, the Equerry and the two Ladies-in-Waiting.

They both spoke very little English, but were quite fluent in French, which made it easy for Titania to converse with them.

The Captain and the other two

male passengers had a great deal to say to each other and they were talking about the role British Battleships played in the Mediterranean and whether it was still important, as it had been some years earlier, for them to patrol the Aegean Sea.

Titania knew that when the Russians were infiltrating the Balkans and threatening Constantinople, Queen Victoria had sent five Battleships into the Straits and the Grand Duke Nicholas had been forced to move his forces back, losing a great number of Russians on the way.

In addition the reverse had cost the Russians a great deal of money which they could ill afford at the time and was the main reason why they dared not provoke Great Britain into war.

Because Titania was a woman, the three men did not draw her into their conversation, but she listened carefully to what they were saying and found it all extremely interesting.

Her father and mother had always talked intelligently to her as they were both wrapped up in the political situation of the different European countries and other places in the world they themselves had visited.

Titania had found the conversation at Starbrooke Hall very dull and uninteresting.

The Duke, who spoke very little, would occasionally complain about the farmers and workers on his estate as well as deprecating the lack of game birds as being the fault of the gamekeepers, but at least he did approve of the number of his horses in foal.

The Duchess, unless the servants were in the room, was continually moaning about the staff. She found the younger members frivolous and careless and those who had been at the Hall for many years she said were growing lazy.

Titania was not expected to join in with this sort of conversation nor did she want to. She merely thought miserably of the interesting discussions there had been at home between her parents, who had invariably let her join in and express her opinions.

There was always some new book just published, which her father found enthralling and he received many letters from his friends in Egypt, India and Japan.

Invariably he had an anecdote or story about the country concerned which made Titania and her mother laugh.

'I wish Papa was with me now,' mused Titania. 'It would be so helpful if he had been to Velidos and could have told me all about the country.'

When dinner was finished she went up on deck. It was twilight and the stars were just coming out and a new moon was creeping up the sky.

She was leaning over the rail when the Equerry joined her.

"What are you thinking about, Miss Brooke?" he asked.

She had learnt over dinner that his name was Darius.

"I was thinking it is fascinating to be at sea again, but I wish I was going to a country I knew something about."

"What do you want to know about Velidos?" Darius enquired.

"Everything you can tell me," replied Titania eagerly. "Its history, its people and of course its King. I know very little about him."

"I find him a most interesting man," said Darius slowly as if he was choosing his words carefully. "But at the same time he is very little known to the people of Velidos."

Titania looked at him in surprise.

"What do you mean? Surely as King he must have a large role to play in the development of his country."

"I am afraid not," answered Darius. "King Alexius is a very intelligent man, but extremely reserved and that is why his people know very little about him. Even those like myself, who serve him, find it is difficult to break down the barriers with which he surrounds himself."

Titania became interested.

"That seems strange. I never thought of a King being like that. In fact in most countries they are very busy and continually in the public eye."

"I wish I could say the same about Velidos. King Alexius is almost a recluse."

"What does he do? What is he interested in?"

"He is writing a book at the moment on the history of Velidos, which is actually, as you have just said, very little known to the outside world."

"That is helpful at any rate," Titania said. "But surely if he is writing a book about his country, he must be interested in it."

"I think as far as his book is concerned he is only at the beginning, when hundreds of years ago Velidos was part of Greece."

"I had no idea."

"It's true and of course the people in those days obviously accepted the Greek philosophy and their belief in their Gods and Goddesses."

"I want to believe in them now," Titania told him. "That of course is what your King must give his people."

Darius laughed.

"I doubt if His Majesty would accept such a suggestion, even if you had the chance of making it."

"Are you saying it is difficult to see the King?"

"He finds the luncheon and dinner parties which take place at the Palace extremely boring. He prefers to dine with one other Equerry and

myself and while we are very privi-
leged and it is most interesting for
us, I often wish those who criticise
him could understand what he is
feeling and thinking about his
country."

Titania was intrigued. This was
something she had never expected
to hear and was certainly different
from any Royalty she had visited
when she had been travelling with
her father and mother.

"Tell me more about the King,"
she begged.

"I do not want you to become
interested in him," replied Darius,
"and then be disappointed. I find
him an exceptional person and it's
only because he isolates himself
from the ordinary people that I feel

he is making a mistake in the way he is reigning Velidos."

"Have you told the King about your feelings?" enquired Titania.

"I doubt if he would listen to me. He has chosen his way of life and left the Crown Prince to take over many of the duties which should be his."

Because Titania was very perceptive, she realised from the inflection in Darius's voice that he did not like Prince Frederick.

"I suppose," she said a little tentatively, "what you are saying is that, since there is no Queen, my cousin will have a great deal to do."

"Perhaps she will enjoy it. I only wish the King would take on some of his duties and get to know the people who are alive in Velidos now rather than those who lived there hundreds of years ago."

"I suppose he finds research very absorbing," commented Titania. "My father undertook a great deal of research before he visited the countries which interested him. As soon as I was old enough I used to help him."

"And then you travelled with him?"

"I have been to a great many places in the world, which is why I do not think I will find it very difficult to learn your language."

"We will start your lessons tomorrow," Darius promised, "and of course I will be a very strict teacher. You will have to work very hard if you are to speak fluently by the time we arrive."

Titania knew he was teasing her. He clearly thought it would be quite impossible for her to learn a language in so short a time and it made her even more determined than she was already that she would speak Velidosian fluently.

She was looking out to sea, aware that the moonlight was now turning the water to silver and the night held an enchantment that was difficult to put into words.

She was not thinking of him, but she suddenly became aware that Darius was looking at her.

"You are very lovely, Miss Brooke," he murmured, "and as we in Velidos love beauty, I promise you that you will be a great success in our country."

Titania smiled at him.

"It is very kind of you to say anything so encouraging, but I doubt if I shall be allowed to meet many of your people or, as I would like to do, explore the country."

"Why should you not do so?" he asked.

Titania thought quickly that it would be a mistake for him to re-alise what an unpleasant position she occupied in the family to which she belonged.

"I think," she said at length, "that I must retire to bed. My aunt will be displeased if she hears I am on deck talking to you and of course unchaperoned."

"Now you are making difficulties," protested Darius. "I assure you most people take such matters of etiquette more easily at sea and forget all the social restrictions that are so important on land."

"I only hope you that are right and I don't wish to be forbidden to take my lessons with you. I must therefore go and ask both my aunt and my cousin if there is anything I can do for them before I retire to bed."

She put out her hand as she spoke and added,

"Good night and thank you for saying you will teach me what I want to know."

"It is an honour and a privilege," Darius replied.

To Titania's surprise he raised her hand to his lips and kissed it.

"Good night, Miss Brooke. I am looking forward to our first lesson tomorrow."

Titania left him, thinking he was very kind and friendly. If all the people in Velidos were like him, it might make life easier than she had expected it to be, but equally there were still Sophie and her aunt to cope with.

She went first to the cabin occupied by the Duchess.

"I have come to say good night, Aunt Louise," ventured Titania, as she entered.

"You should have come to me earlier," the Duchess told her sharply. "What have you been doing? I heard that dinner was over at least an hour ago."

"I have been on deck."

"Alone?"

"The Equerry spoke to me before I came below."

"Now you will kindly behave yourself while I am tied to my bed and cannot keep an eye on you. If I find you flirting with that young man or anyone else, I will make you stay in your cabin and lock you in until we arrive. Is that clear?"

For one moment Titania wanted to tell her aunt she would not be spoken to in such a fashion.

As her father's daughter she knew how to behave herself properly, but then she knew only too well there was no point arguing with her aunt.

She merely responded,

"I assure you, Aunt Louise, that I know how to behave as I have been at sea many times with my father."

At the mention of Lord Rupert, the Duchess sniffed, but did not say anything. She merely looked round the cabin as if she was trying to find something to find fault with.

Finally after a pause she said,

"Give me my glasses. They are on the dressing table and then you had better go to bed. I have told Martha when I wish to be woken tomorrow morning."

Titania brought her aunt her glasses and walked towards the door.

"Good night, Aunt Louise. I hope

you sleep well."

The Duchess did not answer.

Titania left closing the door quietly behind her and then moved on to Sophie's cabin.

Sophie had obviously enjoyed a good dinner and was in a better temper than she had been when they first came aboard.

"What is happening?" she asked Titania. "Did you have a dreary dinner with those awful old women?"

"It was not very exciting, as the three men talked amongst themselves and obviously did not intend a woman to join in."

"Just what I expected," grumbled Sophie. "It's going to be a very boring journey until I meet Frederick."

She paused for a moment and then asked,

"What is that Equerry like? He at least is young and not bad-looking."

"I think he was sent," answered Titania slowly, "so that he could teach you Velidosian before you arrive."

"If that is what he has come for, he's going to be disappointed. I have no wish to learn their silly language and although I would not mind talking to him, Mama would be horrified at the idea of his sitting at my bedside."

Titania laughed.

"I am afraid she would!"

"In which case he will have failed in his mission," snorted Sophie.

"As I have already said, I am not going to learn any language other than the ones I know already."

Titania looked round the cabin.

"Is there anything you want," she asked, "because I am going to bed."

"I expect I shall want a lot in the morning," replied Sophie, "but I cannot think of anything now. As soon as you know I have been called, Titania, you had better come to see me. It would be a mistake for you to have nothing to do while we are at sea."

"Yes, of course. Good night, Sophie, sleep well."

Her cousin did not bother to reply and she walked to her cabin, which was quite comfortable and very much the same as Sophie's.

She felt that at least the Captain believed she was someone of importance whatever her relatives might think.

As she undressed she wished with all her heart that her father and mother were with her on the voyage.

It would be to some country where her father knew there was a Monastery to visit where no Englishman had ever been or it might be to a town that had recently discovered treasures dating back to the early times of civilisation.

There was always something new and something thrilling to arouse Lord Rupert's attention and interest. It would make him determined, no matter how difficult the journey, that he would see it before anyone else did.

'I must look out in Velidos for what is unusual, just as you would have done, Papa,' mused Titania to herself as she undressed. 'I hope to get the chance to see the King who sounds interesting, even though he is isolating himself from the modern world.'

When she climbed into bed she thought of Mercury and she was certain that tomorrow morning he would be waiting for her and think it strange when she did not come to the stables at seven o'clock as she always did.

She had explained to him why she had to go away and hoped that he understood.

'There is no one else except Nanny and Mercury who belong to me now,' she told herself. 'And this ship is carrying me further and further away from them.'

She felt the tears come into her eyes and with an almost super-human effort she prevented herself from crying.

'I will have to be brave,' she lectured herself. 'I have to explore a new country and somehow lead a new life despite Sophie, who will try to stop me from doing so and enjoying myself.'

It was then that she remembered she had managed to obtain five hundred pounds to put into a bank in Velidos.

She had not told her uncle the

truth as to why she wanted the money. The real reason was that if she could not bear being alone in a strange land, she would be able to run away and return home.

'It is just a precaution!' she had told herself and at the same time she knew it was really a way out.

CHAPTER THREE

The sea in the Mediterranean was calm and blue.

Nevertheless the Duchess said she preferred to remain in her cabin and Sophie said the same and it seemed extraordinary to Titania they should not want to look at the beauty all around them.

There was the great Rock of Gibraltar, glimpses of the Northern coast of Africa, then the island of Malta and finally the many Greek islands in the Aegean Sea and the

Eastern coastline of Greece.

All of these sights thrilled Titania.

Even while the ship was pitching and rolling in the Bay of Biscay, she had managed to attend her lessons with Darius.

They had laughed when the books slipped off the table and found it amusing when it became so rough that it was easier to sit on the floor than on a chair.

Darius was astonished how quickly Titania assimilated the Velidosian language and she seldom made a second mistake if he had corrected her.

When he praised her, she admitted,

"I am really a fraud, Darius, because I do know Greek and I find that nearly every other word of your language has a Greek origin."

"I know His Majesty will never believe it when I tell him that one member of the party from England can speak our language fluently," Darius told her.

"It is something the King wishes us to do?"

"He considers it very important for Lady Sophie to be able to speak her husband's language and, of course, he did not know that you would be aboard."

Titania thought that would not be of much interest to him anyway.

Aloud she said,

"I only hope we make a good impression when we do arrive."

"I can assure you, you will do so,"

replied Darius.

She smiled at him thinking how kind he was, but she was always apprehensive that her aunt would discover she was having lessons with him.

Titania was quite certain that, if the Duchess learnt she was sitting for hours alone with a young man, she would put a stop to it immediately, but at that moment she was feeling far too ill to worry about anything.

Sophie was in the same state and this enabled Titania to be with Darius almost the whole day.

When their lessons were over they went out on deck. Darius managed to procure a mackintosh coat for her from one of the seamen and it covered her from top to toe.

They watched the waves splashing over the bow of the ship, jumping to avoid those which would have soaked them to the skin if they had not been quick enough to get out of the way.

It was all great fun and they laughed a lot and Titania was now a little less unhappy at leaving Mercury.

She was, however, afraid that everything would be changed when they reached the Mediterranean.

The two Ladies-in-Waiting crept into the Saloon for luncheon, looking very pale and still suffering from seasickness.

"How is it possible," the elderly Minister of State asked Titania, "that you enjoy the sea and are apparently stimulated by it rather than collapsing as your relations have done?"

"I have led a very different life from theirs," Titania told him. "I travelled with Papa and Mama when I was practically in the cradle. So I have become immune to all the difficulties and problems that other people endure when they leave solid English soil."

He laughed at her remark and the way he looked at her told Titania that he admired her. It gave her a happy feeling she had not enjoyed since she had gone to live with her uncle.

Whilst they were passing along the Northern Coast of Africa, Titania was still having her lessons, which had now become conversations rather than bothering with grammar and the pronunciation of words.

"Do you suppose," Titania asked of Darius, "there would be any chance of our visiting Greece? I would so love to see again all the places I love so much that I feel I really belong to them."

Darius smiled.

"I am glad you feel like that and it is certainly something which will please the King."

"Why particularly him?"

"I thought you knew," replied Darius, "that the King's mother was Greek."

"No one told me that, but I did

not think that Prince Frederick looked in the least like a Greek."

"He has no Greek blood in him."

"I don't understand." Titania looked puzzled.

"It's quite easy really," Darius told her. "King Stelos, who was the present King's father, married a Greek Princess. She was very lovely and they were blissfully happy, but sadly when their son, Alexius, was only three years old she died."

Titania was listening and found it fascinating what Darius was telling her and thought it was important information that her uncle should have told her and Sophie before they left for the journey.

"Under pressure from the Prime Minister and the Cabinet," continued Darius, "King Stelos married again and this time it was a German Princess who, from what I have seen from her portraits, was not at all beautiful and like so many Germans very bossy."

Titania now realised why she had not liked Prince Frederick and thought he gave himself unwarranted airs.

As his mother had been German she could understand why he boasted about his achievements and he treated everyone he met as if he was very much their superior.

"I think," Darius was saying, "that our present King had an unhappy childhood and that could account for the fact that he now does what he wants to do regardless of what his Cabinet says."

"I am sure they are always telling him that he must make public appearances and speeches," said Titania. "It is what some Royalty enjoy, but I have always thought it could become very tiresome."

Darius did not answer and after a moment she added,

"At the same time if his people need him, then he should try to help them."

Darius chuckled.

"Now you are being very English and playing mother to the poor little countries like ours, which you have taken under your protection. You are also determined that we should make the best of ourselves."

"Is that what you think the English do?"

"I have seen them doing it," replied Darius, "and, as you know, no one does it better than your Queen Victoria!"

"I have heard her called the *Matchmaker of Europe*," remarked Titania. "I suppose in the same way, because she is so old and so important, she does seem to some countries like a *Mother Superior.*"

"That is exactly the right word for it," agreed Darius and they both laughed.

The Battleship passed Sicily and was drawing nearer to Greece.

At last the Duchess and Sophie aroused themselves to dress and appear at luncheon. It was then, for the first time, that they asked the Ladies-in-Waiting to tell them about the arrangements for the wedding.

The Minister of State explained who would be meeting them on their arrival.

"There will of course be His Royal Highness Prince Frederick," he told Sophie, "the Prime Minister, the Lord Chamberlain and members of the Council."

After a pause he continued,

"There will be two speeches and, Lady Sophie, you will be presented with a bouquet by a child dressed in our national costume."

"I hope I do not have to say anything," enquired Sophie, looking worried.

"It would be very much appreciated if you could say a few words," the Minister of State answered. "I am sure that if I write them down you would find them quite easy to pronounce."

"If I speak, I speak in English," stated Sophie, tossing her head. "And if people cannot understand me it is their own fault."

The Minister of State looked somewhat disconcerted and Darius offered,

"Do let me help you, my Lady, at least to say thank you in Velidosian."

Sophie hesitated and then because Darius was a good-looking young man she suggested,

"Let us go and sit in a shady place on deck and I will try to learn just two or three words of your language, although actually I think it quite unnecessary."

"I am sure if you will do so," said Darius tactfully, "you will delight our people. And you do realise, my Lady, there will be very large crowds to see you arrive and to cheer you all the way to the Palace."

This made Sophie think about her appearance.

Titania was made to unpack a great number of different hats and dresses as now Sophie was determined to look outstanding when she arrived at the port.

It was planned that the ship should appear at exactly eleven o'clock. Allowing time for it to dock and the gangways to be let down, the welcome should commence at half past eleven.

The Duchess was equally concerned with her own appearance and made nearly as much fuss about it as Sophie.

Nobody gave a thought to what Titania would be wearing for the occasion, but she was thankful that Nanny had insisted on her buying a few pretty and expensive dresses from London.

"First impressions are always important," her mother had once told her.

Titania therefore put on her best afternoon gown and her prettiest hat trimmed with flowers.

"Do I look alright, Martha?" she asked the Duchess's maid, knowing no one else would be in the slightest interested.

"If you asks me," replied Martha, "you look too pretty, Miss Titania, for it to please her Ladyship."

Titania smiled.

"She is quite safe, Martha. I am certainly not in a position to steal her thunder!"

"Now you try and enjoy yourself," said Martha in a motherly tone, "now you're in a new country. It's a real shame the way they treats you at the Hall and I promised Nanny I'd look after you. So if you're in trouble, you come to me."

Titania was very touched as she had never thought that Martha took any notice of her. She was always in attendance on her aunt and she had hardly ever spoken to her.

"That is most kind of you, Martha, and as you can guess, I miss Nanny terribly."

"I knows she'll be missing you too, but equally she'll want you to have a good time. You're too young to be bothering about other people's importance and the way they grab at everything for themselves. It's something your father and mother never did."

"Thank you for all you have said, Martha. I shall be sorry when you go back to England with Aunt Louise."

"Well you remember what I've

said to you," continued Martha, "and don't you go making yourself too unhappy because you're in a strange country. It's something your father always enjoyed, although His Grace had a lot of disagreeable things to say about him, because he was travelling round the world instead of staying at home with them lot."

"To Papa it was always an adventure," admitted Titania, "and that was what Nanny said I was to make it."

"Well you never knows what might turn up. Perhaps, although you don't think so now, it'll prove to be a blessing in disguise."

"I do hope so and thank you for saying all those kind words to me."

She left the cabin and had no idea that when she was gone Martha shook her head.

'It's a crying shame,' she said to herself, 'the way His Grace and her Ladyship treats Miss Titania. But with her looks she should find someone special to comfort her.'

The next morning everyone was up early making ready for their arrival.

The Duchess was giving her daughter instructions as well as finding fault with Titania simply because she felt disagreeable at being out of bed.

Sophie changed her hat half a dozen times.

"I am sure everyone will think you look wonderful," Titania told her to cheer her up.

"It's Frederick I am worrying about," answered Sophie. "After all there must have been dozens of other women longing to marry him and, as Papa says, there are not many young and handsome Crown Princes lying about! Actually, I am rather lucky to have found one."

Titania had heard stories at Starbrooke that Prince Frederick had originally asked Queen Victoria for an English Princess and the Queen had thought it somewhat presumptuous of him.

"I find it difficult," she had said to the Duke, who was in attendance, "to find enough Princesses for reigning Monarchs in Europe and a Crown Prince cannot expect, when his brother is so young, ever to be King."

"That is perfectly true, ma'am," commented the Duke.

He had then paused before he had added somewhat nervously,

"May I remind you, ma'am, that my daughter Sophie is eighteen and is to be presented to Your Majesty this Season."

The Queen had stared at him,

"But of course, Duke, you are absolutely right. Prince Frederick would be very lucky to marry into your family, which is one of the oldest in England and I hear that your daughter is very attractive."

Titania had learnt what had been said from Nanny, who had been told it by Martha as she had heard the Duke telling his wife the story when he returned home.

They had forgotten that Martha was in the room, or what was more likely, Titania thought, had imagined as so many employers did that their servants were blind, deaf and dumb.

The story had of course quickly gone round all the senior servants of the household, who thought that Lady Sophie was very fortunate to make such a brilliant marriage.

Only Titania thought that it was rather sad with Sophie being just second fiddle for a Crown Prince who could not catch a Princess.

Prince Frederick, dressed in a spectacular uniform covered in medals, was waiting for them when the ship came into port.

He was the first person to step aboard and Sophie was waiting for him in the Saloon.

For a few minutes they were allowed to be alone and then they were joined by the Minister of State, the Ladies-in-Waiting and Darius.

The Duchess made an almost dramatic appearance just before they were to go ashore and Titania was allowed to walk behind her.

Prince Frederick kissed the Duchess's hand and gave Titania a slight nod as she curtsied to him.

Then he helped Sophie down the gangway to where the Prime Minister and other dignitaries were waiting to greet her. Only they were allowed near the dais where Sophie was being received.

When they started to drive towards the Palace in open carriages, Titania could see a little of the City for the first time and the people who lived in it.

It was as beautiful as had she expected and the streets were lined with trees in blossom.

The crowds around them were waving the flags of Velidos and the Union Jack and there were children with posies of flowers who ran to give them to Sophie. When the carriages did not move slowly enough, they threw their flowers after them.

The procession was led by a troop of Cavalry and a band on horseback.

It was certainly all very dramatic and Titania was certain it had all been carefully arranged by Prince Frederick himself.

She expected the Palace to look attractive, but it was in fact out-standingly beautiful. It was situated on one side of the City halfway up a small hill and there was a long flight of steps up to it with foun-tains on either side.

What Titania had not expected but could now see in the distance were lofty mountains, their peaks still white with the snows of winter.

She did not know why, but she had expected Velidos to be a flat country and now she could see the mountains, she realised the country would be even more appealing than she had anticipated.

There was also a profusion of flowers in the Palace gardens and as the trees on the route were in blossom it made the whole drive seem enchanting, especially with the music coming softly from the band riding ahead.

Sophie was in the first carriage with the Crown Prince, the Prime Minister and the Lord Chamberlain, while the Duchess travelled in the second carriage with two dignitaries and the Minister of State who had travelled with them from England.

Titania was left with Darius and the two Ladies-in-Waiting.

"Now," said Darius to her, "you are seeing Velidos at its best. There are, I am afraid to say, very much poorer parts of the City and the people find it hard to scrape a living."

"Surely there are products that you make here which could be sold to other countries," asked Titania.

"It is difficult for us to think what our people can do and nothing grows that is easy to export."

Darius spoke as if it worried him and then added quickly,

"But of course there is nothing you can do about it, Miss Brooke, and I should not be troubling you or your cousin with such matters."

By the way he spoke, Titania knew he was thinking it would be quite useless to discuss this subject with Sophie.

She had been aware when Sophie appeared after her seasickness that Darius had looked at her eagerly and had even gone out of his way to talk to her whenever he had an opportunity, but he soon learned that Sophie never listened to anyone unless they were talking about her and her own concerns.

After three or four attempts to tell her about the country where she was to live, Darius had given up.

The procession moved slowly on and Titania could see that many of the children lining the route were poorly dressed. Some wore no shoes and were bare-footed and others had torn and ragged clothes which hardly covered them.

"Are you a poor country?" she

asked Darius, thinking it was a question that she should have asked him earlier.

"We never seem to have enough money for our needs, but it is not anything that can be easily changed. I have talked to the King about the problem, but like everyone else he cannot think of anything we can export. We can only just manage to feed ourselves."

'There must be something,' Titania thought and wished her father was with her.

She remembered how he had made suggestions to countries they visited about improving their wealth and prosperity and often they had followed his ideas and found them very successful.

She thought that the Crown Prince with German blood in him would be ambitious enough to want Velidos to stand out amongst the other small Balkan States.

However she had gained the distinct impression that he was too busy enjoying himself to worry about the poor and unemployed.

'Perhaps I am being uncharitable,' she corrected herself, 'but I fear that Sophie will find him a very self-centred man who will not trouble unduly about anyone except himself.'

At last they reached the Palace and Prince Frederick led Sophie up the long flight of marble steps covered in a bright red carpet with the rest of the procession following closely behind.

Titania found the fountains enchanting and the flowers growing around them were more colourful than anything that could be seen in an English garden.

But when they entered the Palace, Titania was somewhat disappointed.

It had been cleverly sited with a magnificent view over the City and the mountains in the distance, but the furnishings were rather dull and ordinary. There were not the many beautiful pictures and treasures of china and silver that she had anticipated.

She had been in quite a number of Palaces one way or another and most of them, especially those in

India, had been filled with treasures that thrilled the eye and which she had often longed to possess.

In contrast this Palace seemed almost austere and then she remembered that the last Queen had been German.

Now she understood that everything she was seeing fulfilled all necessities, but there were no frills or furbelows to delight the mind and the imagination.

The party proceeded to the Throne Room, where a large number of guests had gathered to greet the Royal party.

Prince Frederick took Sophie onto the raised platform in the middle of the room and when everyone was seated, he made a long speech of welcome.

There was nothing very original in what he said, Titania thought. He made it quite plain how clever he had been to win such an important bride from England with the approval and blessing of Her Majesty Queen Victoria.

He next added many flattering words about the Duchess and her aristocratic family and indeed it would have been more appropriate if he had not made it quite so clear that it was he who was bringing them to Velidos. In fact he was expecting Velidos to be very grateful to him.

It was a long speech and, as he droned on and on, Titania thought he was being extremely tedious, but it was worse still for Sophie who did not understand a word of what he was saying.

It was not surprising that her cousin looked bored and started to fidget towards the end of the speech.

Finally Prince Frederick brought the account of his achievements to an end and he bowed delightedly to the polite applause from his captive audience.

Next the Prime Minister made his speech of welcome and he was followed by several other dignitaries.

By this time Titania was feeling really sorry for her cousin.

They were all speaking in a language of which she had only learned two words and these she had already uttered when the child had presented her with a bouquet.

Titania, however, was delighted to find that she could understand everything being said. Even so she considered that the speeches were too solemn and certainly far too long.

At last the interminable speeches came to an end and Titania was wondering what would happen next.

Then there was a fanfare of trumpets, a door opened at the end of the Throne Room and two Equerries appeared.

It was obvious from the fanfare that the King was coming to receive his brother's future wife.

Titania watched eagerly for his

appearance.

From the way Darius had talked about him poring over his books and having withdrawn himself into a world of his own, she had believed he would be small and rather insignificant.

To her surprise the King was tall, broad-shouldered and very good-looking.

He was dressed in quite a plain uniform in contrast to the Crown Prince's, wearing a white jacket with just two glittering diamond stars on one side of his chest.

As he processed into the Throne Room, the men bowed and the women curtsied and then he stepped up onto the platform.

Prince Frederick introduced him

first to Sophie and next to the Duchess, but there was no question of Titania being presented. She was left sitting in the background beside the two elderly Ladies-in-Waiting.

The King then made a very short speech of welcome to Sophie, wishing her every possible happiness in the new country to which she now belonged.

Then as the King stepped down from the platform again the men bowed and the women curtsied.

His Majesty left the Throne Room.

When he had departed, Prince Frederick took over and he and Sophie led the guests into a large Banqueting Hall.

There was plentiful champagne to drink the health of the bride and groom and a number of delicious dishes which Titania had never tasted before.

Everyone who had been present in the Throne Room now wanted to meet Sophie, and Prince Frederick introduced them one after another. They each had something extremely flattering to say to her, but only one in ten was able to speak a word of English.

With the majority Sophie could only look blank and smile.

'Of course she should have tried to learn the language,' thought Titania.

However it was too late now and she was quite certain that Sophie would make no effort once she was married.

Titania remembered Darius had told her it was the King's idea that he should travel with them in the Battleship to teach Sophie the language of the people over whom he ruled.

She wondered now if he would be disappointed that Darius had been unsuccessful or more likely he was not really interested one way or another.

She wished she could have had a chance to meet him later.

She could see the Greek blood in him by the darkness of his hair and eyes and he was certainly taller than the average Greek, and that, she knew, must be due to Velidos.

Looking round at the men in the Throne Room, she had seen they were nearly all well-built and broad-shouldered, something un-usual in some of the Balkan States she had visited with her father.

The men were not outstanding, while the women were extremely pretty, but there were not many women present at the Palace and Titania supposed that the invita-tion had been for those who had important appointments, particu-larly in the Government.

However, the few women she could see were certainly attractive and also quite well-dressed.

There must be quite a number, Titania thought, whom Sophie would find as good friends and she hoped that her cousin would be wise enough to make herself pleasant to them.

Sophie in many ways was like her father, considering that anyone who was not blue-blooded was hardly worth talking to.

At Starbrooke only the most important people in London Society were invited to stay and most of her uncle's friends were Dukes like himself or minor members of the Royal family.

Titania had found the formal, rather pompous parties he had given for such guests extremely dull and she compared them with the parties her father and mother had given in different countries where they travelled.

She had only been a child, but she could remember one all too vividly.

A dinner-party had been given by a neighbour who owned a great deal of land and a number of gypsy families roamed freely over his estate. To amuse Titania's parents, he had asked the gypsies to sing and dance for them after dinner and after the entertainments they had sat down with their host's guests.

They chatted away about their life and told the fortunes of those who wanted to know about their future.

It had been a very exciting party and Titania thought she would always remember the music the gypsies had created with their strange instruments and the way they had sung and danced.

She could not imagine Sophie and the Crown Prince enjoying anything like that.

They would have thought it degrading to join in the strange parties her father had taken her to in Constantinople, where there was belly-dancing and Arabs showing the way they could fight each other without hurting any of those they challenged to a contest.

Titania gave a little sigh.

Any parties that were given at the Palace would, she was certain, be very correct and in fact very boring.

Yet she knew that Sophie would doubtless be happy enough now that she was important. Every woman was curtsying to her and the men were kissing her hand reverently.

It was thus a relief when they could retire to their rooms because, as Prince Frederick said,

"No one is to be tired tomorrow on my wedding-day!"

'That at least,' thought Titania, 'will be an exciting event.'

Even if, as she expected, Sophie would be making a tremendous fuss about everything and she would undoubtedly be run off her feet trying to please her.

Her bedroom was comfortable and well-furnished, but at the same time rather dull, like the rest of the rooms in the Palace.

Titania found that her windows overlooked the front and she could see the steps they had climbed to enter the Palace and had an even better view of the mountains in the distance.

'I would love to ride nearer to those fabulous mountains,' she wished and she was sure that beneath them there would be flat ground for her to gallop over, just as there had been Steppes in Hungary where she had ridden with her father.

She gave a deep sigh.

Sophie would not want to ride and there would be no question of her being allowed to do so.

Once again her mind went back to Mercury and she wondered how he was and she was still thinking about him when there was a tap on her door and Martha put her head round it.

"Her Ladyship's screaming the house down for you, Miss Titania," she told her urgently. "And as I can't leave Her Grace, you'll have to attend to her."

"All right, Martha, I will go at once, but, tell me, what do you think of the Palace?"

Martha shrugged her shoulders.

"It looks all right as Palaces go," she said, "but if you asks me, I'd rather be in a cottage at home than in any swell building in a foreign country."

Titania laughed because it was just the answer she would have expected.

Then she hurried into Sophie's room which was only a few doors away from hers.

"Where have you been?" Sophie scolded her angrily as she entered. "Surely you realise I need you. I have got to change and I have no idea what I am expected to wear. I cannot understand a word the women say who are unpacking my luggage."

Titania was glad to know that there was someone to help and she would not have to do it all herself.

Then she asked her cousin,

"What are we doing this evening? Has no one told you?"

"I believe there is to be a dinner party," Sophie answered, "but at what time and where I have not the slightest idea."

She gave a little scream of frustration as she added,

"Surely you can do something. As you speak the language or think you do, you could ask what is going on."

"I will go and find out at once."

Titania stepped out of Sophie's bedroom and saw with relief that one of the Ladies-in-Waiting was going into a room opposite.

She ran across to her.

"I am sorry to bother you, but my cousin has not been told what is happening tonight and she has no idea what she should wear."

"Oh, there is a big dinner-party," replied the Lady-in-Waiting, "and I think they are hoping the King will come, although that is unlikely."

"And what should my cousin wear?"

"One of her best gowns and of course a tiara on her head."

Titania ran back to Sophie's room.

When she told her what was happening, Sophie said,

"Just what I had expected. At the same time an *aide-de-camp* or one of those men who hang about the place should tell me what is planned and what time the dinner-party will take place."

"I am sure there must be a programme of events somewhere."

Titania ran back into the passage again and now she found a rather harassed *aide-de-camp* hurrying up the stairs.

As he held a piece of paper in his hand, Titania enquired of him as he reached her,

"Is that by any chance a copy of the programme for Lady Sophie? She is worried as no one has told her what is happening this evening."

"I am sorry, I am very sorry," answered the *aide-de-camp*. "I expect I shall be told it is my fault. But no one could make up their minds about anything to begin with and then His Royal Highness Prince Frederick altered everything round at the last moment and we had to have it printed again."

Titania laughed.

"I can understand your difficulties. It is what happens everywhere when there is a big party."

The *aide-de-camp* tried to smile.

"I have been ticked off for being a nincompoop," he told her, "and can only be grateful we do not have a wedding every day of the year!"

"I expect this one will have to last you for a long time. Can I please have a programme too or like you I shall be in serious trouble."

The *aide-de-camp* looked at her as if he was seeing her for the first time and murmured,

"I am sure no one could be angry with anyone who looks as lovely as you do."

He spoke in his own language and Titania smiled.

"Thank you, kind sir, for the compliment. Equally as you well know there is nothing more exhausting than being late and trying to pretend one is on time."

"I will bring you everything that is happening the moment I know it myself," replied the *aide-de-camp*. "And if you get the chance to sooth down Prince Frederick — he is in one of his tantrums."

Titania's eyes widened for a moment, but she said nothing. She merely thought it was just like the Germans to rant and rave if anything went wrong and it must be the German blood in Prince Frederick which was making him behave in such a fashion.

However, it was a mistake to

waste time speculating and so she hurried back to Sophie with the programme.

"And about time too," snapped Sophie when she saw her. "Frederick has told me that if he has the chance he is going to make this country run more efficiently. But I understand they are trying to prevent him from doing so, simply because they like their lazy easy way of going on."

Titania made no comment.

She only thought, although of course she could never say so, that she disliked Prince Frederick and she was sorry that Sophie would have to put up with him for the rest of her life.

CHAPTER FOUR

The wedding day started badly.

Sophie struck Titania with a hair-brush, because her hair under her veil was not as she wanted it.

It was the first time she had ever done so and it made Titania angry, but despite her indignation she considered it was unwise to make a scene on this particular day.

She therefore re-arranged Sophie's hair and thought it was almost the same as it had been before.

Then they went down to the hall, where the Lord Chamberlain was waiting to escort Sophie to the Cathedral as Prince Frederick had already gone on ahead.

Sophie had said disagreeably while Titania was helping her to dress,

"The King should have given me away, but he refused. I think it is rather degrading for me to have to put up with the Lord Chamberlain."

"It's a pity Uncle Edward could not come," Titania put in.

"Papa would have hated every moment of it all," grumbled Sophie, "because I am not being treated as grandly as he had expected me to be."

Titania could not think of her being received any more grandly as Sophie had been treated as the most important person present at every function she had attended so far and she would undoubtedly be the focus of attention in the Cathedral.

But Titania had learned it was no use arguing with her cousin when she had made up her mind about herself and always insisted that she was right and everyone else was wrong.

The Lord Chamberlain certainly looked resplendent in his robes and as he was a handsome old man, Titania thought that Sophie should be content.

There was a splendid glass coach

drawn by four white horses waiting to take her to the Cathedral and Titania followed as usual with the Ladies-in-Waiting, but not in the company of Darius.

She now realised that Darius had been sent to travel with them on the ship as a very special concession on the part of the King, who believed it was essential that Sophie should learn the language of her new country.

He had therefore temporarily spared Darius who was his most important Equerry.

Darius would now be entering the Cathedral, Titania was told, with Kastri, his vis-à-vis, the other personal Equerry to the King.

Sophie had been asked if she

would like child bridesmaids to follow her up the aisle, but had refused immediately.

"Children are always a nuisance in Church," she had said, "and I have no wish to have them distracting the attention of the congregation away from me."

Titania knew that the mothers of the children must have already made their dresses and they would be looking forward to their little ones taking part in the ceremony. They would obviously be very disappointed, but that did not seem to worry Sophie.

She complained about her bouquet under her breath to Titania and then swept into the glass coach that was waiting for her at the back of the Palace.

If she had gone out of the front entrance, she would have had to walk down the steps and this she had refused to do.

"I don't mind climbing up the steps once we are married," Titania heard her tell Prince Frederick, "but I am not going down alone with no one to support me."

"You will have the Lord Chamberlain," Prince Frederick had answered, looking surprised.

"I will go on your arm or nobody's," asserted Sophie, tossing her head.

At first Titania thought Prince Frederick was rather pleased with the compliment, but his lips tightened as if his impulse was to tell

Sophie she was to do as she was told.

Titania could not help reflecting that he would find Sophie very difficult to manage once they were married and then she told herself that Germans usually had quiet placid wives and she suspected that was what Prince Frederick expected Sophie to be.

As soon as Sophie had driven away in her fairy-tale coach, Titania climbed into the next one and smiled at the elderly Ladies-in-Waiting who were obviously agitated.

Apparently Sophie had told them rather rudely that she did not want then to intrude on her and at the reception that would follow the ceremony and in the Cathedral they were to keep in the background.

This was the way she always talked to Titania, but the Ladies-in-Waiting, however, were flustered and felt insulted by Sophie's peremptory edict.

The sun was now shining brightly and the route to the Cathedral, which was partly the same as their route from the port, was very beautiful.

The same crowds of people were there waving flags and staring at the bridal procession.

As the procession was moving rather slowly, Titania had a chance to look over the heads of the crowd at the shops behind them and was surprised, as she had been told this was the main road of the City, how few shops there were and they seemed to display very inferior articles for sale.

Titania knew Sophie would be disappointed if she could not go shopping as it was something she really enjoyed.

In fact she had said to Titania only yesterday,

"As soon as we have time and I don't have some doleful collection of women calling on me, we will go shopping. I am sure there will be exciting things for us to buy."

Titania knew it was not a question of *us*.

She had no intention of spending what money she had brought with her on frivolities as it was there in case she needed to run away or had some really sensible reason for spending it.

But she thought it would be interesting to visit the local shops, as in many Balkan countries, the women spun, sewed or knitted delightful garments to be sold to tourists.

'I must take Nanny back some really nice gift,' resolved Titania, 'but there is no one else who will expect me to bring them anything.'

Then she wondered miserably how soon it would be before she could go back to England. She so wanted to ride Mercury and have Nanny to look after her again.

Sophie had, of course, been allotted a lady's-maid from the Palace

staff, but as she could not com-
municate with her or give her any
orders, Titania had to be with her
all the time.

On the way to the Cathedral Titania found herself sighing.

While it was a new experience to
go to a Royal Wedding, there would
doubtless be an enormous amount
of work for her to do afterwards.

The Cathedral was very impos-
ing, in fact far finer than Titania
had predicted and it was packed
with what she knew must be the
elite of Velidos, whilst outside there
was a huge crowd of ordinary
people who had come to watch and
applaud.

They cheered Sophie as soon as
she appeared and Titania thought

that at least would delight her cousin.

There were some steps up to the Cathedral and Sophie walked up them slowly so that the crowd could see her elaborate wedding gown. There was a diamond tiara on her head and her veil had been chosen so as not to obscure her gown in any way.

Titania and the Ladies-in-Waiting followed slowly and they discreetly did not attempt to climb the steps until Sophie had actually entered the West door.

They were seated in one of the Royal pews and Titania had a good view of the Cathedral as well as the marriage ceremony.

The King had already arrived and

was seated on what looked like a throne, surrounded by Bishops and other dignitaries of the Church.

Titania thought his appearance was most impressive.

'He certainly looks a King,' she mused, 'even if he does not behave like one.'

The Marriage Service had been chosen, she had been informed, by Prince Frederick himself.

It took a very long time and was very spectacular and when finally the bride and bridegroom had been blessed by the Archbishop, there was a fanfare of trumpets.

Titania was affected by the singing of the choir and by the sincerity with which the Archbishop took the Service.

She only wished that Sophie could understand everything that was said, especially the few quiet words the Archbishop addressed to her and Prince Frederick before he finally married them.

She could tell by the expression on her cousin's face that she was very proud to be Prince Frederick's wife, just as he was exceedingly proud of himself.

It took a long time for all the principals to leave the Cathedral.

Titania and the Ladies-in-Waiting had to wait at the bottom of the steps and it took nearly a quarter of an hour before their carriage was able to reach them.

Whilst she was waiting she looked at the people in the crowd and thought again how poorly dressed and how ragged many of the children appeared.

The women seemed harassed as if they were worrying about their families and she thought that quite a number of people looked as if they did not have enough to eat.

'Surely the King could do something about this,' she thought, as she wondered if she talked to Sophie whether she would understand what was required, but she accepted, however, that this was a hopeless idea.

Not only would Sophie refuse to listen, but she would say firmly that she had no intention of worrying herself about the common people and that if they worked hard enough they should be able to feed themselves.

As Titania drove back towards the Palace she was treated to another glimpse of the snow-peaked mountains.

'It is such a pretty country,' she pondered, 'surely someone should try to make it prosperous.'

She recognised at once that the someone was the King.

Yet if all she had heard about him was the truth, he was interested only in the past and not the present.

And another aspect of her situation she found very depressing was that there was no bookcase in the boudoir, which opened out of her bedroom and she had thought at first it was rather exciting to have a sitting room all to herself, but then she realised that unless she was writing a letter, there was nothing else for her to do.

'There must be books somewhere in the Palace,' she reasoned.

She had asked the *aide-de-camp* who was sitting next to her at dinner if there was a library.

"We do have a very large and very important library," he replied, "but I doubt if you will ever see it."

"Why ever not?" asked Titania in surprise.

"Because His Majesty works in the library," answered the *aide-de-camp*. "He likes to keep his reference books all around him and that of course means that no one must disturb him."

"But surely there are books elsewhere in the Palace."

"I cannot think of any at the moment," the *aide-de-camp* told her, "but I will try to find out for you. You sound as if you are an avid reader."

"I love books," enthused Titania.

At the same time she thought if she could not read there would be very little to do, except of course to listen to Sophie's endless complaints and to try to cheer up the fraught Ladies-in-Waiting.

She thought of the enormous number of books her father had kept at home and they would have been hers if her uncle had not sold them all with the house, although she had to admit that the library at Starbrooke Hall was very comprehensive.

She thought now that if the worst came to the worst she would have to buy books in Velidos, even if it meant spending some of her precious money.

Amid the cheers, waving of flags and throwing of flowers by the children, the procession eventually reached the steps of the Palace.

Now holding on to Prince Frederick's arm Sophie was only too pleased to walk up the steps and they stopped halfway to turn and wave to the crowds before reaching the top.

The other carriages coming from the Cathedral drove round to the back of the Palace and there was, much to Titania's surprise, no sign of the King in the procession.

She learnt later that he had left the Cathedral by a side door and had then been taken back to the Palace by a different route where there were no crowds.

'I expect,' Titania thought, 'he does not want to steal any of the glamour and applause from his brother.'

Equally she could not help wondering if there was a different reason and perhaps the King was bored by all this fuss and excitement over a wedding.

Titania reasoned to herself that this could be true.

The bridal couple, having arrived

at the Palace, processed straight into the Throne Room to receive their guests, but there was still no sign of the King.

Titania watched her cousin shaking hands with hundreds of people before moving into the great Banqueting Hall.

Prince Frederick cut the cake with his sword and everyone drank their health.

Titania had learned, although the rest of the guests were unaware of any such arrangements, that the bride and bridegroom were not going away on a honeymoon.

As Sophie had just spent a long time at sea, she had no wish to board a ship again and the Prince was anxious for her to stay in the

City and be seen on a great number of different occasions.

When Titania looked at the programme, she thought it seemed rather boring, but she was sure that Sophie would enjoy being the most important person present.

After the wedding-breakfast was over Prince Frederick made yet another much shorter speech and then the bride and bridegroom bid everyone farewell and retired to their own suite, where they were to be left strictly alone and not disturbed by anyone in the Palace.

Titania, of course, was required to help Sophie change from her wedding dress into a different gown.

"Everyone admired you, Sophie,"

she said as she took off her tiara, "and you must have felt proud to be of such importance to so many people."

"I thought my bouquet should have been larger," moaned Sophie, "and if I had realised I was to wear my own tiara, I would have brought one of Mama's larger ones."

"Did you expect Prince Frederick to give you one of the Crown Jewels?"

"Why not? I am one of the Royal family now and, as there is no Queen, undoubtedly the First Lady in the land is *me*."

She said it so proudly that Titania was quite certain that Prince Frederick had put the idea into her head, as she would not have thought of such an idea herself.

"Of course," continued Sophie, "you must be aware that Frederick should really be King instead of his brother, who behaves as if he is a monk or a recluse."

She spoke scornfully.

"He looks very different from what I had expected," admitted Titania, "and he is certainly very handsome."

"I don't admire him at all," scoffed Sophie, "and, if you ask me, the best thing he could do would be to abdicate in favour of Frederick!"

Titania felt that this was a dangerous way of talking and she hoped it was the sort of remark that Sophie would say only to her and to no one else.

She was just about to ask her cousin to be careful with her words when Sophie changed the subject.

"I intend to get hold of some of the Royal Jewels," she said. "I have heard they are fantastic. But Frederick told me that when he suggested it to the King, he said they should only be worn by the Queen and, of course, I am not that — *yet.*"

It struck Titania as rather a strange comment to make.

She could understand, however, that Sophie resented that the King had paid her so little attention and he certainly should have attended the wedding celebrations after they had returned to the Palace.

Sophie disappeared into Prince Frederick's suite and Titania found herself alone.

Once again she longed for a book to read and she knew it was no use looking in her boudoir. She had also searched the much larger and more impressive room which adjoined Sophie's bedroom and again there was no bookcase.

Finally when it was time for dinner, she walked downstairs.

She found the two Ladies-in-Waiting and the Lord Chamberlain in one of the smaller dining rooms, but there was no sign of Darius, who she guessed would be in attendance with the King.

The Prime Minister and the other dignitaries from the City had all left and she ate a rather solemn dinner with very little conversation.

Titania was glad when eventually she could retire upstairs to bed.

It took her a little time to get to sleep and she dreamed that she was back at Starbrooke riding Mercury over the fields.

She woke early and after a long night's sleep she had no wish to stay in bed as she was used to riding Mercury at seven o'clock in the morning.

She wondered now if she could find the Royal stables and see what kind of horses the King owned, but she quickly realised if she did so without being escorted by an *aide-de-camp,* it would be deemed a breach of protocol and she would certainly be reproved by the Ladies-in-Waiting.

So she walked downstairs and as she entered the hall, she saw a postman handing over a large amount of letters and parcels to one of the footmen.

Titania thought the parcels were undoubtedly presents for Sophie, but she wondered if there might be a letter for her.

There had not been one from Nanny when she arrived which had rather surprised her.

She waited until the postman had left and as the footman put the parcels and letters down on a table, she walked towards him.

"Good morning," Titania greeted

him speaking in his language. "I wonder if there is a letter for me from England."

The young footman smiled at her.

"Let me have a look," he said, addressing her by a word which she knew meant, 'my Lady.' "

Because she was impatient, he did not seem to mind when she turned over some of the letters and at last she noticed one with an English stamp. It was addressed to her and she picked it up and showed it to the footman.

Then she walked out of the door into the gardens at the back of the Palace which she had not yet seen and found them to be very exotic with a profusion of flowers every-where.

There were almonds and many other fruit trees in blossom and huge flowerbeds of Madonna lilies as white as the peaks of the mountains Titania could see through the trees and there was an exquisite sculpted fountain playing in the centre of the lawn.

When Titania walked on a little further, she found to her surprise a terrace and steps leading down to a small lake. She guessed it had been constructed at the same time as the Palace and it too was very beautiful.

She sat down on a marble seat beside the lake and opened her letter.

It was from Nanny and Titania had been so longing to hear from her as it would tell her news about Mercury.

She read what Nanny had written and read it again and then she put her hands up to her face and started to cry.

She could not help it nor could she stop the tears from running down her cheeks.

She felt as if the sky had crashed down on her head and that the whole world surrounding her had become darkened.

Then unexpectedly a man's voice behind her asked,

"What has upset you? Why are you crying?"

She thought it was Darius and without answering she picked up the letter which lay in her lap, turned and handed it to him.

She covered her face again and tried to control her tears.

She became aware that Darius had sat down beside her and was reading the letter.

Titania felt as if the words were burning in front of her eyes.

Nanny had written,

"My Dearest Miss Titania,

I have been to see Mercury every day as I promised you I would. He misses you very much, as I do, and the stable boys tell me that at seven o'clock every morning he's waiting at the door of his stall expecting you to come in from the yard.

They're exercising him as you'd want them to do, but at the same time he won't eat his food and has got a little thin. He's so pleased to see me and nuzzles against me, but he wants to be with you.

Now I have some bad news although I don't want to upset you. His Grace sent for me last night and said that now you've gone abroad there's really not enough work for me to do at the Hall. He therefore suggested I should find other employment and he gave me a month in which to do so.

You knows as well as I do, dearest, that I've never been with anyone except you and your dear mother, and I don't know how to begin to serve anyone else.

I'd go to my own family, but I've lost touch with them these past years and have no idea where I can find them.

I expect I'll be all right, but I am really too old to start a new life all over again.

I'll write to you again in two days time as I promised, and I'm sure Mercury will be better by then.

Take care of your precious self and God be with you.

Your loving, Nanny."

Titania had heard the rustle of the paper as Darius turned the letter over.

Then a strange voice said,

"Stop crying and let us discuss what we can do about this problem."

Titania was astounded that it was not Darius beside her and she took her hands away from her eyes and turned her head round.

To her amazement she was look-ing at the *King*!

He was gazing at her and she had no idea how pitiable yet at the same time how lovely she looked.

There were tears in her large grey eyes running down the soft white skin of her cheeks.

"I — thought — you were — Darius, Your — M-Majesty," she managed to stammer.

As she spoke she began to rise and curtsy.

The King put out his hand and laid it on her arm.

"Do not move," he said. "I have read this letter from your Nanny and of course it is something you cannot allow to happen."

"What — can I — do?" asked Titania in a broken voice. "My uncle said I would — only be — here for six months and I had — no idea he would — send Nanny away. She is getting on for sixty and it is — cruel and wicked of him to make her — try to find somewhere — else to work."

"I agree with you," said the King. "That is why I will suggest a solution which I am sure you will agree with."

"I thought," murmured Titania tentatively, "that perhaps — you would — send me home. If I was back in England — Uncle Edward would have to let — Nanny stay with me, and if he grudges her money — I have some of my own, but he has — control of it."

"I have a much better idea than that."

"What — is it — Sire?"

As she spoke she realised she had not yet addressed him correctly, so she added quickly,

"I am sorry I am not — being very polite, but it is difficult to think of — anything but the two people in the world I have, who — love me as I — love them."

"Why are there so few?"

"It is a long story which I am sure would bore Your Majesty," she answered.

"I want to know," insisted the King. "Darius told me that you are at the beck and call of your cousin and your aunt."

"They are ashamed of me and to punish me for what my father did, Uncle Edward is sending Nanny away — and I am terrified that he may now sell my Mercury."

"I am sure no one could be so cruel as to do that," the King told her firmly. "But what I am going to suggest will prevent him doing anything so wrong and from sending your Nanny away."

Titania tried to wipe away her tears.

She did not have a handkerchief and so the King drew a white linen one from his pocket and handed it to her.

She rubbed her eyes and looked at him pleadingly, wondering what he could possibly suggest, feeling there was nothing that would prevent the Duke from doing what he wished to do.

"You were telling me why you are treated so badly by your relations?"

"Because Papa, when he was a young man, fell very much in love with my mother. She was very beautiful, but her father was only the Chieftain of a Scottish Clan. My grandfather believed that all his family must marry into families who were as important and blue-blooded as his own."

The King smiled.

"I have heard there are English aristocrats who feel that way, but I thought it was just a fairy story."

"No, Sire, it is not and Uncle Edward is just like his father. Nothing to him is more important than one's ancestry and that is why they do not consider me as anything but a blot on the family tree."

The King smiled again.

"I am sure no one could think of you as a blot on anything. You are very beautiful, as you must be aware, and I do not like to see anyone in my household in tears, especially someone who looks as if she might just be a Goddess from Mount Olympus."

Titania could not help giving a little laugh.

"Like your Majesty's mother!" she exclaimed. "I have been told how very beautiful she was and that she was Greek."

"I can only just remember her

because I was only three when she died. But I know exactly what you are feeling, because my stepmother never liked me. She was angry that I should be more important to the country than her son."

"Was she unkind to you?" asked Titania, remembering that the Queen in question had been German.

There was a little pause before the King said,

"I understand from this letter that you love your horse Mercury and he loves you. I once owned a dog that I adored. In fact after my mother died he was the one thing I had to love and who loved me."

Titania drew in her breath.

There was a note of pain in the

King's voice, which she understood only too well.

"What happened?" she enquired almost in a whisper.

"When I was sent to boarding school, I could not take my dog with me. But I asked all the servants to look after him and they promised me they would do so."

"So what happened?" asked Titania again.

"As he whined and barked continually because he missed me, my stepmother had him destroyed."

Now his voice was hard, but Titania could see the pain in his eyes.

"I am so sorry. I know how much it — must have hurt you. I now am frightened that my Uncle Edward, because he dislikes me, may dispose of Mercury. I think I would rather he died than he was sold to someone who — might ill-treat him."

"I agree with you there and it is something we must definitely prevent."

"How can we do so, when I am here and Mercury is — in England?"

The King chuckled.

"I am going to send a cable now to my Ambassador in London instructing him that I personally wish a horse called Mercury and —"

He paused.

"What is your Nanny's name?"

Because she was listening to him so intently, Titania found it hard to answer for a moment.

Then she said,

"Tucket — Miss Tucket."

The King continued,

"— that he and Miss Tucket be sent immediately to His Majesty in Velidos."

Titania clasped her fingers together.

"I do not believe it," she sighed. "I must be dreaming."

"What I have said is the truth and I will also send a cable to your uncle, making it very clear it is a Royal Command that your horse and your Nanny should join you immediately."

For a moment Titania could not speak and then as the tears came back into her eyes she said,

"How is it possible that — you could be — *so kind?*"

"You can thank me when they arrive in Velidos, and as that will take a little time, I suggest you try out my horses and see how they compare with yours."

"Do you mean I can — ride with — Your Majesty?"

The King pulled his watch from his waistcoat pocket.

"It is now ten to seven," he said. "I will give you exactly ten minutes to meet me in the stables. Darius will wait for you in the hall to show you the way."

Titania jumped to her feet.

"You are the most — wonderful King that ever existed," she enthused. "But I do not believe — you are real."

She did not wait for the King to

answer, but she heard him laugh as she ran across the garden and back towards the Palace.

It was fortunate that Titania was used to dressing and undressing quickly.

She rushed into her bedroom and to her relief she found that the maid who was looking after her had hung up her riding habit in the wardrobe.

It only took her a minute or so to put it on and then snatching up her hat with its gauze veil she left the room and ran down the stairs.

Darius was waiting where she expected to find him in the hall.

He smiled at her and said,

"I thought you would break the record and if we run, the King will be surprised how quick you have been."

Even as he spoke they started to run down the long empty corridors and left the Palace by a side door that led directly to the stables.

When Titania arrived at the stables she saw the King inspecting a horse equipped with a side saddle and knew it was for her.

As she reached the King he looked round in surprise.

"You are certainly much quicker than I had reckoned! An example to every other woman I have ever met!"

Titania smiled at him.

"I hope, Sire, you have chosen a spirited horse for me."

"I would not insult you with anything that was not as fast as mine," the King answered.

Titania thought she would have to mount from the mounting-block, but to her surprise the King put his hands on her waist and lifted her onto the saddle.

As she picked up the reins she reflected that this was something she could never have expected.

Yet it was one of the most exciting adventures that could have happened to her.

The King mounted quickly.

As they rode side by side to the end of the stables, he told Titania,

"The horse you are riding came from Hungary. And, as I am sure you know, Hungarian horses are internationally famous."

"I have seen them and ridden them."

The King looked surprised.

"You have been to Hungary?"

"I travelled to Hungary with my father about six years ago and I realised then what I had heard about the horses had not been exaggerated. It was fascinating to ride over the Steppes."

"I had not expected you to be a traveller, Miss Brooke."

"And I had no idea, Sire, that you are a magician and could sweep away my unhappiness with just a touch of your magic wand!"

The King laughed.

"I have been called many things, but never a magician!"

"I can think of a lot of other

names for you, but I know this must be a dream and I shall wake up crying, as I was when Your Majesty found me."

"It is something you will never do again," he asserted. "I like you when you are smiling and pretty. Women should never cry."

"Nanny said that it made me look ugly, so I will definitely try not to do so."

"I doubt if anything could make you look ugly. In fact you make the world lovelier just because you are in it."

He paid his compliments in a sort of dry unemotional voice, which did not make Titania feel at all embarrassed, but she did wonder if he was really laughing at her for making such a fuss.

Then as they moved swiftly over the low ground she looked back to see that they were followed by two horsemen. She could not see them very clearly, but she was sure that one of them was Darius and guessed the other would be Kastri.

As if she had asked him a question the King informed her,

"I am not allowed to ride without an escort, but I tell them to keep as far away as possible because I like to feel free and unencumbered."

"Am I not preventing you, Sire, from feeling so this morning?"

"It's a new experience. You may think it strange, but this is actually the first time I have asked a woman to come riding with me."

"Then I am most flattered, Sire, but I think my Nanny would say it is very bad for you not to be more sociable."

She thought as she spoke that she had been too daring and the King might take offence.

Instead of which he said,

"I expect your Nanny is right, but at the same time I like doing things the way I want to do them."

"Like writing a book?"

"So you have heard about that?" exclaimed the King.

"Darius told me that is what Your Majesty is doing."

"And I suppose, like most people, you think that it is a terrible waste of time."

"No of course not!" cried Titania. "You are setting down the history of your country and it is something that should have been done years ago. But equally there are other matters which should also interest you, Sire, because they need your brains and, as I have found, your very kind heart."

The King looked at her in surprise.

Then as if he did not want to answer her, he suggested they race each other for the next half mile.

The ground they were riding over was flat and there was a river running down one side. Just ahead the mountains rose up high above them.

As Titania rode towards them she

could see how stunning they were, but for the moment she needed to concentrate on racing the King.

Her horse, which was almost as fine as Mercury, was only too willing to compete and it was the horses that set the pace as they strove to outride each other.

Only when they drew them both in did Titania say,

"I think, Sire, you won, but only by a head."

"You ride better than any woman I have ever seen and that is more than a compliment, it is the truth."

"Thank you, Sire, and actually I was thinking the same about Your Majesty, but was too shy to say it aloud."

"I think," suggested the King, "if

we are going to ride like this every morning until your horse arrives, we should be frank with each other and forget the protocol."

"Did you really say that I could — ride with you every morning?" asked Titania breathlessly.

"I will see that you have a horse that is worthy of you and I cannot believe that it will interfere with any of our other duties if we leave at such an early hour."

It was then that Titania came back to reality as she had forgotten everything in the excitement of riding with the King and being mounted on one of the most spirited and swift horses she had ever experienced.

She looked at the King and

whispered,

"I am — frightened."

"What of?"

"If my cousin learns that I am riding with you, she will — forbid me to do so. I am sure that — my aunt will not — allow it."

"I think if we are clever," the King told her, "there will be no reason for anyone except Darius and Kastri to know that you accompany me on my morning ride. They can deal with the other servants effectively and you can be back and ready when Princess Sophie requires you."

"That is clever, so very clever of you!" exclaimed Titania. "And now that I have had this wonderful ride with Your Majesty, I would miss it madly if it has to stop!"

"Then that is certainly something we must prevent."

The King drew his watch from his pocket.

"Now we must turn back and ride home."

Titania took a last look round as she rode beside the King.

She thought it was all too marvellous to be true and she was riding a horse that was almost as good as Mercury.

Yet because the King was so kind, Mercury would be with her in a short time as well as Nanny.

'I am happy, I am so happy,' she said to herself, 'I want to kiss the whole world!'

CHAPTER FIVE

The King and Titania reached the
entrance to the Palace grounds a
little in advance of the two *aides-
de-camp,* who had kept well behind
as they were told to do.

As they drew in their horses the
King said to Titania,

"I am sure you will be in plenty
of time, but why do you have to be
with your cousin so early in the
morning?"

"Because," replied Titania, "she
has a lady's maid who does not

speak English, so I have to translate everything she requires."

The King put his hand up to his forehead.

"I never thought of that! But it is something that can easily be remedied."

Titania looked at him questioningly.

Then she said to the King,

"It seems wrong for me to ask you for anything when you have been so wonderful — but there is something I do want very badly."

"What is it?" the King asked.

"Some books to read."

The King looked surprised and Titania explained,

"There does not seem to be a book in the whole Palace except in the library and you know, Sire, that is forbidden ground!"

The King laughed a little ruefully.

"That is something else I never thought of, but, of course, you shall have some books. What do you want — novels?"

"I can think of far more interesting books I want to read, especially about your wonderful country."

She thought that she caught a slightly cynical twist to the King's lips and added quickly,

"My father always took immense trouble to learn about a country before he visited it and then he did as much research as he could when he was there, besides of course meeting as many of the people as possible."

"You shall have exactly what you want," the King promised her.

As the two *aides-de-camp* joined them, he said to Kastri,

"You are to immediately find a lady's maid for Princess Sophie who speaks English, as I understand that the one who has been provided speaks only our language and that is not, I consider, very hospitable."

Kastri looked as if he thought the King considered that it was all his fault, but His Majesty had already turned his head towards Darius.

"When Miss Brooke is free of her duties," he ordered, "take her into the library so that she can choose whichever books she requires. I understand there are none in her sitting room or anywhere else in the Palace."

"I think, Sire," replied Darius, "they were put away with the ornaments and all the other superfluous *objets d'art* when Your Majesty's stepmother became Queen."

"Do you mean they are all preserved in some part of the Palace?"

"Yes indeed, Sire, there is quite an Aladdin's cave in some of the rooms that are never used."

"I think one day soon I shall have to explore them," the King reflected.

He then rode on with Titania beside him until they reached the stables.

As she knew it must be approaching nine o'clock, she slipped from the saddle down to the ground and said to the King who had also dismounted,

"Thank you again, Sire, thank you, thank you from the bottom of my heart! I have no other words to express what I feel."

She did not wait for an answer, but ran across the cobbled yard towards the back door which led into the Palace.

The King watched her until she was out of sight before giving orders to his Head Groom as to which horses he would require the next morning.

Titania ran upstairs to her bedroom.

She could hardly believe that what had happened was not part of a glorious dream, but she knew that Sophie would make a great fuss if she heard about her adventure and so she changed quickly into her morning dress.

She next walked into the boudoir where her breakfast was ready for her.

She ate swiftly, but there was no need to do so as it was nearly an hour before Sophie sent for her.

When she reached her cousin's bedroom, she found that beside the lady's maid whom she already knew, there was another in attendance.

Sophie was addressing the newcomer in English and the woman was then being told by the Velidosi lady's maid what she had been told the day before and had put out the clothes that Sophie required.

"Oh, there you are, Titania," Sophie called as her cousin entered the room. "I have been supplied with a new lady's maid who speaks English and I suppose it's better late than never."

"I am sure it will be much more comfortable for you," said Titania in a low voice.

"You can supervise her to save me the trouble of explaining what I require," Sophie told her in an uncompromising voice.

But she did not sound as disagreeable as she usually did in the morning and Titania could only hope that she was happy in her marriage.

A little while later a message came

that Prince Frederick had arranged for Sophie to drive with him into the City, where they were to receive a special wedding present from the Velidosian Members of Parliament which they had not been given the previous day.

Sophie was immediately in a tizzy, insisting on looking very smart and tried on several hats before she was satisfied with her appearance.

When she was told that the Prince was waiting for her, she hurried downstairs.

Titania gave a sigh of relief and went to her boudoir, hoping that Darius would soon appear to take her to the library.

She was not to be disappointed.

He came into the room after

about five minutes and she jumped up from where she was sitting.

"Is it safe for me to visit the library now?" she asked Darius.

"Quite safe and I will take you a special way which will avoid the footmen on duty in the hall from seeing you."

"We sound like conspirators," Titania smiled at him.

"As it happens," Darius told her, "I think that is what we actually are. I assure you that everyone at the Palace would be absolutely amazed if they realised you were being allowed to interrupt His Majesty when he is working in the library."

"I had to ask him if I could have something to read," explained Titania. "I could not sit here doing nothing but twiddling my thumbs all day."

Darius laughed.

"I cannot imagine you sitting around being idle and I am sure we can think of various ways to keep you amused."

Titania did not answer, thinking it was not amusement she needed but occupation.

Darius took her down a side staircase and they walked along several deserted passages. Finally they reached the library which was situated at the other end of the Palace.

Titania was taken in through a different door from the one which was used by other visitors, Darius told her.

One glance at the library told her it was absolutely magnificent and indeed it was exactly as she hoped it would be.

The upper shelves near the ceiling were reached from a balcony with a balustrade consisting of an elaborate tracery of gilded flower-leaves.

There must, Titania conjectured, be thousands of books in the room.

Then she saw the King's large writing-desk just in front of the door Darius had taken her through and he was sitting at it writing with his back to them.

Yet without Darius speaking he became aware that they were behind him and rose to his feet.

Titania remembered to curtsy

and said excitedly,

"This is the most magnificent library I have ever seen! How lucky you are to have all these marvellous books."

"That is just what I think," agreed the King, "but I have never met anyone else who was particularly enthusiastic about them."

"I think they are wonderful and I would like to read every single one!"

The King laughed.

"I am afraid that will take you a very long time, though of course I shall only be too delighted for you to be my guest for at least a hundred years!"

Titania laughed too.

"Now what particularly would

you find of interest?" he enquired.

"I was wondering what you are working on at the moment," replied Titania.

She had noticed as she entered the room that there was a huge pile of books by the desk and several ancient tomes open on the desk itself.

"As I expect Darius has told you that I am writing the history of Velidos. I discovered only a short while ago that one of the Kings a century or so ago was interested in religion. He therefore invited representatives of all the great religions at that time to come to Velidos and tell him of their beliefs."

"That is a subject that would have fascinated my father."

"At the moment," the King continued as if she had not spoken, "I
am researching a religion I am sure
you have never heard of — that of
the Sufis."

Titania gave a little laugh.

"Certainly I have heard of them,
Sire, and actually I met and talked
to a number of Sufis when we were
travelling in the Middle East."

The King stared at her as if he
thought it was somewhat unlikely.

Titania continued,

"I am sure you have many books
in this amazing library about the
mysticism of Islam, and, of course
as you will know, the Sufis have a
fascinating store of legends and stories."

She looked at the King waiting for

his comment, but he merely nod-
ded,

"Go on."

"They have, Papa thought, raised
poetry to the highest level of aspira-
tion and, what I found more exciting, brought song and dance into
the lives of artisans and peasants."

The King sat down in his chair.

"I do not believe it!" he exclaimed. "You cannot be saying all
this to me. I have never met anyone
in Velidos who knows anything
about the Sufis."

Titania smiled.

"Who else came to your ancestor's meeting, Sire? Perhaps I have
heard of them too."

The King looked down at his
papers in front of him and she felt

he was deliberately choosing one of the more difficult religions before he responded,

"The Zen Buddhists for one. What do you know about them?"

He spoke as if it was a challenge.

"I have been to some of their monasteries and was thrilled with the stonework they carved to describe what they felt about 'the wisdom that has gone beyond.' "

She paused for a moment.

"Papa, of course, was allowed to go inside the monastery, which I was not, but he did write down some of the stories they told him that he found extremely interesting."

"I would like to see your father's notes."

Titania made a helpless little gesture with her hands.

"I was not allowed to keep them, but I might have saved one or two of them at home. My uncle sold my father's house and all its contents and that included all the notes he had written about our journeys abroad."

There was a hint of pain in her voice which the King did not miss.

"Tell me about the other religions you encountered when you were travelling with your father."

"Of course, when we were travelling I was very young," Titania told him. "But I feel that a great deal that went into my mind at the time will come back to me. We visited Egypt, and I longed to know the secrets behind the Sphinx! I remember being thrilled with the Pyramids and the long arguments between the experts as to why and how they were built and what exactly they meant to the Egyptians themselves."

"Egypt interests me too," admitted the King.

Titania was thinking before she added,

"I know of one very strange religion that might have been represented at your ancestor's conference, but most people know very little about it."

"What is that?"

"It is what Papa called *the Wisdom of the Forest*," Titania answered.

As she spoke she saw the King look at her even more incredulously.

"It was in the forests of India that men meditated and sought for union with the *World Beyond the World.* We talked to some of the Indians who had suffered tortures from the heat and the cold as well as wild animals and insects in the deep forests, where they attempted to master all the powers that transcend the Universe."

She spoke the words dreamily.

She was remembering how she had seen the ascetics in question and what they had said at the time. Then feeling as if perhaps she was talking too much, she looked at the King questioningly.

"I think," he said, "that you have been sent to me like a messenger from the Gods to help me just as I was feeling I had come up against a brick wall. And I should like from now on to address you by your Christian name."

"That is very gracious of you, Sire, my name is Titania and I will help you if I can, but as I said I was young at the time, perhaps only fifteen, when we met those who were seeking wisdom either in the perilous mountains or in the depths of the jungle."

"What you have said already, Titania, is a tremendous help to me, and I want you to search through your mind for what you think you may have forgotten, but which I am sure you can find again."

Titania laughed.

"Now you are talking in the way some of the Priests and devotees talked to Papa. It sounded very grand, but it all boiled down to one thing — they wanted to improve themselves and to rise from the world they were living in into something more sublime."

"I think that is just what we all want," commented the King.

"Not everyone unfortunately —"

She was thinking of her uncle and aunt who were completely content with themselves exactly as they were.

"Now you have to help me," proposed the King, "but in the meantime I can offer you in return the freedom of my library. Come when you like, take what you like, but please while you are searching for yourself, search as well for anything that you think will help my book."

"Of course, Sire, I would be delighted, and as it means so much to you I am sure it will help a great many other people."

She was not certain as she spoke whether the King had that idea at the back of his mind or not.

She was trying to make him see, as her father would have done, that he must lead a practical life with and for his people, as well as soaring up into the clouds in search of the unknown.

She thought, however, it was a mistake to say anything so provocative so soon.

Instead she walked towards the spiral steps which led up to the balcony.

"Can I go up the steps?" she asked.

"I was going to suggest it, because books in which you are particularly interested are on the top shelf at the far end."

"Then I must look and see if there are any volumes that I have read before, but if they are in your language then I am going to find it hard work."

"I can hardly believe it, when Darius tells me how quickly you have learnt to speak Velidosian so fluently."

"I wish that was true," answered

Titania. "But much of your language is very like Greek and I have spoken Greek ever since I could toddle."

"I don't believe it," the King exclaimed, "unless of course Darius was right when he told me that you are undoubtedly a reincarnation of one of the Goddesses from Olympus!"

"I have never aspired as high as that," smiled Titania.

She had reached the balcony by this time and was looking down at the King.

Again it flashed through his mind how lovely she was.

Her fair hair was shining against the dark covers of the books behind her and he felt he would not be surprised if she vanished and was not real, but just a figment of his imagination.

He watched her as she moved along the balcony.

She occasionally put out her hand to touch a book very gently as if she treated it with reverence.

The King tried to go back to writing his book, but instead he found himself waiting for Titania to turn round to speak to him.

It was a long time before she finally leant over the balcony.

"I have seen three books here, Sire, which I am very anxious to read. One is about Zen Buddhism, so that I can talk to you about it later. May I take them with me?"

"I have already told you, Titania,

all I have is yours."

"That is a very Eastern way of talking, Sire. Beware lest I take you at your word!"

He noticed as she smiled that there were little dimples at the side of her mouth and it made her even more entrancing.

She walked along the balcony carrying three large books bound in red leather and the King reached up and took them from her before she reached the last of the steps.

"Now I must leave you, Sire, because I know I am interrupting your work and that is something I am told you very much resent."

"Not when someone is helping me as much as you are," responded the King. "I want you to read those books, Titania, and then come and tell me exactly what you have learned from them and what would be of interest to me."

"I am beginning to become worried that Your Majesty is expecting too much of me and I would hate you to be disappointed."

"I have a feeling that I shall not be disappointed. Incidentally I have already sent the cables to your uncle and to my Ambassador and I am hoping that both Nanny and Mercury will be with us as quickly as possible."

"How can you be — so kind? And how can I tell you, Sire, how — grateful I am?"

"There is no need for words. I think we are both aware that the

Gods we are seeking have brought us together."

"I can only hope that is true and thank you, Sire, thank you again and again."

She curtsied and went out of the door behind his desk.

She found that Darius was waiting for her and he took the books from her arms.

"I am glad you found something to interest you."

"There are a million books in there to interest me, Darius, and as I read very quickly, please do not let the King forget how much I need something to occupy my mind."

"I should have thought there was plenty of knowledge in your mind without books," remarked Darius. "I wonder whether you would like to see the City this afternoon."

"I would love to."

"I will take you after luncheon," Darius told her, "but I am afraid you will be very disappointed if you expect it to be like London or Paris or any other great Capital City.

"I will tell you what I think after I have seen your City," Titania promised him.

She was relieved that there was no sign of Sophie or Prince Frederick at luncheon and she learned later that because they were on their honeymoon they were having their meals in their own Suite.

She therefore ate with Darius, Kastri and the two Ladies-in-

Waiting.

When they heard that Darius was going to take her to see the City, they insisted that one of them must accompany her.

"Of course, if you want to come," agreed Titania quickly, "it will be delightful. There will be no need for you to keep getting in and out of the carriage as I want to do. You can keep an eye on me quite well without over-tiring yourself!"

She saw a look of relief cross the older woman's face.

She found out that they had both had a very tiring morning following Sophie and having to stand most of the time.

Titania drove with Darius into the City and noticed again that the shops were very few and not at all enticing. In fact there seemed little or nothing to buy.

She was once again entranced by the trees in blossom and the flowers which seemed to grow in unexpected places, but she was shocked by the ragged and bare-footed children, and the dilapidated state of some of the houses off the main streets was a disgrace.

Titania thought it was pointless to say anything and yet she wondered again why nothing was being done to bring prosperity to this beautiful country.

When Titania returned to the Palace, Sophie sent for her to explain to the new lady's maid which gowns she usually wore and exactly what the arrangement of her brushes and combs should be on her dressing table.

There were a dozen other small requirements which Sophie could quite easily have explained herself.

"I hope you are behaving yourself," Sophie said to Titania before she left her suite. "You are not to go out with any of the *aides-de-camp* unless you are accompanied by a Lady-in-Waiting."

"They will find it rather tiring to follow me around as well as you," suggested Titania.

"In which case you must stay in the Palace," Sophie snapped.

It was a great relief to get away from Sophie and be able to curl up on the sofa and read her books.

There were certain passages she longed to discuss with the King and yet she could not help thinking he was only being polite in saying she could help him.

'He is obviously very clever,' she told herself, 'and why should he bother about me?'

However, she could not go to sleep without wondering if the King had forgotten he said they could go riding at seven o'clock.

Had he really meant the invitation or was it just politeness?

The next morning she felt apprehensive when she dressed even earlier than was necessary.

She walked down the back passages which led her out of the

Palace and into the stable yard, where the Head Groom greeted her.

"You're early, miss," he said in his own language, "but yesterday His Majesty chose the horse you are to ride."

Titania's heart gave a little leap — so the King had not forgotten and they would be riding together as she had hoped.

She walked into the stables to see the horses being saddled and was very impressed with the one that the King had chosen for her.

It was a large stallion which the Head Groom told her had come from Hungary and Titania could see that it obviously had Arab blood in it.

She was discussing the horse with him when the stable boy announced that the King was outside.

The horses were hurriedly taken from their stalls and as Titania had expected, Darius and Kastri were with the King.

After she had curtsied to the King, she smiled at the *aides-de-camp* and they bade her good morning.

"I am going to take you for a different ride today," the King told her as they set off. "I think it is important for you to see the different parts of my country."

"It is all exceedingly beautiful," sighed Titania, "and I am so impressed with the high mountains."

"I will show you those on another

day. Now I want to race you as I did yesterday and I think it is what our horses are hoping for."

They rode for quite a long distance at a very fast pace and when they drew in their mounts and were able to speak to each other, the King said,

"I think you will find this part of the country is a little more inhabited than where we were yesterday. There is a small village over there which I have always thought is most picturesque."

"Oh, do let me see it, Sire," begged Titania.

The King smiled good-humouredly and they rode towards the village.

As he had said, the village was

picturesque and built of small houses and there were a few small shops, much to Titania's surprise, but they were empty compared to the ones she had seen yesterday in the City.

She drew her horse up outside one shop that sold furniture beautifully inlaid with mother-of-pearl with different woods that made every piece a real work of art.

"I have never seen anything so pretty!" exclaimed Titania.

Even as she spoke a man who was doubtless the creator of this lovely furniture came out from the back of the shop bowing respectfully.

"Is your furniture for sale?" Titania asked him.

"It is indeed, madam," he replied.

"But alas we have very few visitors to this small village."

Titania looked at the furniture again and then she had a sudden idea.

She turned to the King and speaking in English so that the man could not understand, she suggested,

"This is exactly the sort of shop you should have in the City. The shops there are empty with almost nothing on sale and I can quite understand why you do not have many tourists in Velidos, beautiful though it is."

The King looked at her in astonishment.

"I suppose you are right," he admitted. "Now I come think about it, there is very little to interest a tourist."

Titania turned to the man who was looking at her curiously.

"Are there any more brilliant craftsmen like you in this village?" she asked.

He gave a laugh.

"We are refugees, madam. Our families escaped when the Turks were fighting the Serbs and we were very scared."

Titania remembered that twelve years ago in 1876 the Turks had invaded Serbia and they had been appallingly cruel in the way they fought and treated those they conquered. Everyone in England, including Mr. Disraeli, the Prime Minister, had been horrified at the way they had behaved.

"We escaped and came here," the man was saying. "My sister and her husband have a shop just a few yards up the road where she makes beautiful lace. I know, madam, she would be very proud to show her work to you."

Titania found that he had not exaggerated.

The lace was exquisite and there was a great deal of it because, as the maker said pathetically, there were very few buyers.

There was another shop owned by another relation of a man and his wife who made toys for children. Some of them were carved and some were sewn together from odd pieces of material.

Every one of them was fascinating and Titania knew that they would delight any child.

She praised them and then she turned to the King,

"Alongside the shops in the main street of the City which had so little to sell, I saw several empty ones, which Darius told me had not been occupied for many years."

The King rode back to the first shop, dismounted and looked at the furniture carefully and by this time Darius and Kastri had caught up with them.

Darius held the bridle of Titania's horse as she slipped down to the ground to join the King.

"I have never seen such beautiful work," she exclaimed. "You know how clever the people in some of the Balkan countries are and how many sightseers visit their countries more for what they can buy than for what they can see."

"I know exactly what you are saying to me," muttered the King.

He called to his side the man who had carved the furniture and his relations who had followed them and then he said to them,

"I have a proposition to make to you. I think your brilliant talents are wasted here where, as you say, too few people visit. I want you to move into the City, where there are several empty shops on the main street. I will guarantee that you pay no rent until you can afford to do so after the first year or two. I am convinced that if you continue to work as cleverly as you have done here, you will soon have more customers than you can cope with."

He smiled as he finished speaking and the man's sister who made the lace came forward.

Going down on her knee in front of the King, she kissed his hand.

"You have saved us," she said. "How can we ever thank you enough for making such a proposal to us?"

"Are you quite sure, Sire," the man with the toys said tentatively, "that you can afford to let us have the shops without paying you rent?"

"I see you do not recognise me. I am actually the King of this country and I think you will find there will be no difficulties, except that you will have to decorate the shops to make them look attractive enough for what you have to sell."

It was obvious that the people listening to him were stunned by what the King had said.

Without him and Titania being aware of it, a small crowd of people from the village had seen their horses and out of curiosity they had come to find out what was happening.

Then they understood what was going on and the King learned that there was a man who made the most delicious sweetmeats for children.

Another married couple produced

basket-work and they ran home to fetch some to show the King and it was exceptional.

"I think there will be enough unoccupied shops for all of them," said Titania excitedly.

"I will tell you what I will do," suggested the King. "As soon as I return to the Palace I will send someone who will inform me exactly what is available, and arrange for those of you who wish to be transported to the city to be taken there as soon as possible."

He paused before he added,

"In the meantime I wish to buy six pieces of this beautiful furniture, enough lace to cover a gown for this lady and twenty-five toys which will be left at the Palace."

There was a gasp first of astonishment and next they were almost
incoherent in their thanks and
gratitude.

As they rode away, Titania turned
to the King.

"You have made those people
very happy, Sire. They will serve
Your Majesty faithfully and, of
course, love you for the rest of your
life."

To her surprise the King did not
speak for a moment and then he
replied,

"You must not fit me into a role
for which I am not suited."

"I don't know what you are saying, Sire."

"Ever since I came to the throne,
I have been a King without a heart

and now it is too late for me to change."

"You are nothing of the sort," responded Titania without thinking. "Why should you think that is what you are?"

"It is what I want to be and what I intend to remain."

They rode on for a little way until when they were some distance from the Equerries and Titania asked him,

"You must explain to me. I am feeling somewhat bewildered by what you have just said."

She thought for a moment that the King was going to refuse to talk to her anymore and then he answered,

"When I found you crying yesterday, I told you I understood only too well what you were feeling."

"Because you had lost your dog?" murmured Titania.

"Not only my dog, but everything I have ever cared for. When my mother died I had a nanny who must have been rather like yours. When I was six my stepmother sent her away and replaced her with a young woman who was German like herself. She was told to make a man of me and I was more or less drilled from morning to night. Then, when I grew a little older, she was replaced by tutors who did exactly the same thing."

"I cannot bear to think about it," said Titania in a low voice.

She thought, however, that the

274

King had not heard her as he continued,

"When Frederick was born, my stepmother hated me because I was the heir to my father's throne and not her own son."

"It must have been terrible for you," sighed Titania sympathetically.

"Everything I did was wrong, but I had my dog and he was something to love and he loved me."

"Then you lost him?"

"When I came back from school and found him gone, it was then that I began to think I would never give my heart or my love to anyone again."

"How could anyone be so cruel and so unkind to a young boy?"

"My stepmother was determined that I should have no friends. If I brought home a school friend, he was laughed at and scorned and my stepmother made certain he was never asked again."

He gave a little laugh which had no humour in it before he resumed,

"You can imagine that if I was interested in a girl, what happened. But I soon learnt to avoid anything feminine, because it would be humiliating if they showed an interest in me."

"But eventually you escaped. Your father died and you became King."

"I became King and the first action I took was to send my stepmother back to her relations in Germany. But you can understand that by this time I had learnt the lesson she taught me and I had no intention of ever being as miserable as I had been since my mother died."

"So you pretended, that you — had no heart."

"It was not a question of pretence," the King said sharply. "I have no heart and I have no intention of trying to find one and suffer as I have suffered before in my life."

As he finished speaking he spurred his horse and as he began to gallop Titania had to urge her own mount on to keep up with him.

They rode back to the Palace too quickly for there to be any chance of further conversation.

Only as they rode into the stable yard did Titania say a little nervously,

"You will not forget those people from the village you promised to help?"

"I may not have a heart," replied the King in a cold voice, "but I keep my word and do not go back on it."

"I am sorry, Sire," muttered Titania apologetically, but he was not listening.

He dismounted from his horse which was being held by one of the grooms and without speaking to Titania again, he walked towards the Palace and disappeared.

Titania felt as if the sun had gone

in and the world had become dark.

She had been very proud and delighted when he had been kind to the people in the village. He had solved not only their problems, but had given the City the beginning of the renaissance it so desperately needed.

But now he seemed to be angry with her and she wanted to run after him and apologise again

But as she dismounted Darius was beside her.

"That was very clever of you," he said. "The people are very grateful and the whole City will be astonished and delighted that the King is at last taking some interest in them."

"But surely the Prime Minister

and his colleagues realise that if they want tourists to spend money here, they must have something to attract them."

Darius smiled.

"I suppose being men it is something they never thought of. But of course you are right and I think you are wonderful."

Titania could see the admiration in his eyes.

"But the King is angry with me."

Darius shook his head.

"I don't think so. I believe that he has wanted to do the right thing by his people for a long time, but has prevented himself from doing so because he wishes to remain aloof, so he tries to be entirely immersed in his books rather than in life itself."

"You now think he might change?" Titania questioned him.

"I believe you have made him take the first step and that is the most important. It is the first drop of water that can become a flood, which is what we need."

"I am still worried in case I have upset him," murmured Titania.

They were walking towards the Palace by now and she was still feeling as if the sun had gone in and the King was really angry with her.

As they reached the door, Darius offered,

"If you want to change your books I will come and tell you when the coast is clear."

"Thank you," said Titania and ran up the stairs to her room.

Sophie might be sending for her soon and, whatever happened, her cousin must not find out that she had been riding with the King.

'Perhaps it is something I will never do again,' she thought forlornly.

It had been so exciting to be with him, just as she had been thrilled yesterday when he had listened to her telling him about the Sufis, the Zen Buddhists and those who sought enlightenment in the forest.

'Perhaps he will never listen to me again,' Titania told herself and felt like crying.

But there was nothing she could do and so she ate her breakfast alone and then she waited for the summons to come from Sophie.

She was half afraid that when she did go to her cousin, she would have learnt what she had been doing, but instead Sophie only wanted to tell her what Frederick had planned for her that afternoon.

"We are going to inspect a Battleship," she told Titania, "and Frederick is very anxious that it should be named after him."

"Will the King allow it?"

Sophie gave a derogatory laugh.

"Who cares what he says. Anyway nobody worries about him. All he does is write a stupid book which no one will want to read and it is really Frederick who runs the country."

Again Titania thought this sounded rather dangerous talk, but her cousin rambled on,

"Of course Frederick should be King and I expect he will be sooner rather than later. The people are fed up with a King they never see and who is obviously not interested in them."

Sophie turned away from Titania to look at herself in the mirror.

"I believe the Queen's Crown is very becoming," she continued smugly. "When I am Queen I shall have the Royal Jewels, which have been collected over the centuries and which Frederick tells me are fantastic."

"I think, Sophie, you must be very careful," Titania counselled tentatively. "If people heard you talking like that, they would be — very shocked. After all, the King was crowned and he does rule over this country whatever people may say about him."

"He does nothing, absolutely nothing," Sophie came back positively. "It is Frederick who inspects the troops, what there are of them, encourages the people who are building the Battleship to give it his name and who is cheered whenever he appears in public."

Titania thought the cheers at the wedding had not seemed as spontaneous as might have been expected.

But there was nothing further she could say to Sophie.

She therefore started to talk about

what clothes she would want to wear.

As the conversation was now about herself, Sophie quickly forgot everything but her own appearance.

Chapter Six

Titania was miserable.

The following day the King did not come riding with her and she rode alone with Darius and she did not like to ask him why the King was not there at seven o'clock as he usually was.

She enjoyed being mounted on a very spirited horse she had not yet ridden, but it was not the same as when she was with the King.

In the afternoon when Sophie had gone out, Darius took her to the library and it was unoccupied.

Titania selected several books to read, thinking they would be exciting, but somehow her mind kept going back to the King.

She kept wondering how she had offended him.

It was just the same the next day and that night she was forced to admit to herself that she missed the King unbearably.

It was with the greatest difficulty she did not burst into tears.

'I want to be with him, I want to talk to him,' she kept thinking. 'There is so much I can remember, which I am sure will help him with his book.'

But it was no use telling the darkness.

The King seemed to have disappeared!

Sophie and Prince Frederick were extremely busy visiting organisations and people in the City and they also travelled to other towns which were near enough to be reached in no more than one or two hours driving.

Sophie was happy as she believed that all this activity was because her husband wanted to show her to the people and considered it as a great compliment.

However, Titania could not help wondering if Prince Frederick had other reasons for being so much in the public eye.

On the third morning she went to the stables at the usual time expecting to find only Darius.

The King was there.

When she saw him her heart seemed to turn a somersault and the sky was brighter than it had ever seemed.

She was aware, however, although she might have been mistaken, that the King did not look at her.

He merely said politely,

"Good morning, Titania, I have chosen a special mount for you today and I hope you will enjoy riding him."

"I know I will, Sire."

She desperately wanted to tell him how glad she was that he had returned whilst they were riding together, but she thought it would be a mistake to be so gushing.

They set off at a good pace and as usual galloped until they were far ahead of Darius and Kastri.

Today Titania noticed that the King was taking her on a different route. He was heading towards the mountains, which loomed up ahead, magnificent with their snow-touched peaks.

She could not help thinking that they were most romantic and there was something about mountains and woods that moved her. They were part of the spiritual world which both her father and the King were interested in.

Ever since she had been a child she had believed that the woods were full of goblins and fairies, whilst in the mountains there dwelt the Gods and Goddesses.

She wondered now if the King would ever allow her to try to climb some of the mountains and she felt it would be a very exciting adventure.

They galloped for a long way before drawing their horses in to move a little more slowly.

It was then that the King said in what Titania considered was a somewhat cold voice,

"I promised to show you the mountains and now I have kept my promise."

"They are magnificent," answered Titania, "and I wonder if you have ever had them prospected for gold."

The King looked at her in surprise.

"Why should you imagine," he asked, "that there would be gold in these mountains?"

"If you remember," replied Titania, "gold was found recently in Austria and the Russians have produced more gold from their own mountains than any other country in the world."

The King was still looking at her with a strange expression on his face.

She continued,

"Papa told me that gold has now been discovered in California and Australia and I can see no reason why there should not be gold here in Velidos or alternatively copper or zinc, which are also very valuable."

The King made an exclamation

of exasperation.

"Why did I not think of that? Of course you are right and I know perfectly well that there are rich deposits of gold in Libya and in some lands bordering the Aegean, as well as in Persia and India."

His voice became angry.

"How could I have been so idiotic as not to think that there might be gold, or as you say, other valuable deposits of minerals in my mountains?"

He sounded so exasperated with himself that Titania could not help herself trying to comfort him.

"As Nanny always says — 'it is never too late to mend.' "

"You are quite right, Titania, and it is something I shall organise immediately. If we do find enough gold or anything else to help my people, it is you who must take the credit."

"I do not desire any credit, Sire. I just noticed that some of the children were bare-footed and in rags and thought it strange that nothing was being done for them."

"I understand very well what you are saying and I am in fact ashamed of myself."

Because he was so obviously interested, Titania talked to him about the mountains she had seen in other countries, yet it was impossible not to keep referring to the rich gold strikes that had been made in other parts of the world.

She realised that by the time they

had turned for home the King was determined to investigate her suggestions immediately.

She said a secret prayer that he would find what he was seeking and it would bring him happiness and prosperity to his impoverished country.

Time was getting on as they rode back towards the City.

They were not far from away and were travelling very fast.

Suddenly a child rolled down from a heap of rubble where he was playing in front of the King's horse.

With a brilliant piece of riding His Majesty managed to avoid the horse trampling on the child, but he had fallen on some rough stones and was crying in pain.

The King and Titania drew in their horses.

Without speaking Titania handed the King her reins and slipping to the ground, she ran towards the child.

She saw when she reached him that he was a little boy, very poorly dressed and he had fallen on a sharp stone and cut his knee which was bleeding profusely.

She put her arms around him talking soothingly.

"It's all right, you are not hurt, but I expect the horse has frightened you."

Because he was in her arms and he could understand what she was saying, the boy stopped crying, but by this time there was a good deal of blood running down his bare leg.

Titania looked towards the King.

"Can I have your handkerchief please, Sire?"

The King pulled his handkerchief from his pocket and threw it down to her and she wrapped it round the boy's knee.

It was a jagged cut, but nothing that would not heal fairly quickly. Then she picked him up in her arms, looking round to see if there was anyone who had been with him.

There were two other children playing behind the rubble and Titania called them over to her.

"Who is this little boy and where does he come from?"

They told her that his name was

Ajax and he came from a part of the City she had not heard of.

Carrying the boy in her arms, Titania walked to the King and told him what the children had said.

"I think we shall have to take little Ajax home. He will not be able to walk as things are."

"I realise," said the King with a faint smile, "that he is now my responsibility."

He bent down and Titania passed Ajax up to him.

The King placed the boy on his saddle in front of him and waited while Titania managed to remount her own horse with a little difficulty.

The two *aides-de-camp* were still only dots in the distance and there was no point, she thought, in waiting for them.

The King started off, moving slowly so as not to frighten Ajax, who in fact was not in the least scared and gurgled with glee,

"Ajie riding — big horse — very big — horse."

There was no doubt he was delighted to be in the King's protection as they rode into the City.

People in the streets stared in astonishment at seeing the King with a small boy on the front of his saddle.

Ajax was clean, but his clothes were in rags and his shoes were very old sandals with his toes peeping through them.

The King obviously knew the way

to where Ajax lived and it was no surprise to find it was a narrow street with dilapidated houses on each side. The windowpanes were broken, bricks had fallen from some of the walls and the doors had large cracks in them.

There were a lot of children amongst the crowd in the street and when they saw the King and Titania approach on their fine horses, they stood gaping at them.

They had only ridden a little way down the street before Titania heard someone shout,

"It's the King, I know it be the King!"

The other men and women repeated the words in awed voices and then they all followed the horses.

The King had told Ajax to show him where his home was and the small boy held his arm out pointing ahead.

By the time they reached his house there was quite a crowd of people jostling behind them.

Then as the King drew in his horse, one of the women ran to the door of Ajax's house and Titania could hear her shouting for someone.

A few seconds later a youngish woman came hurrying to the door. She must have been about thirty or perhaps a little older and had doubtless been very pretty in her youth. The hard life and the cares and troubles of a family had made her look older than she actually was.

She stared at Ajax on the King's horse in sheer astonishment.

"Mama, Mama, Ajie riding big horse!" he cried.

The woman who had fetched her out said in what should have been a whisper but was very audible,

"It's *the King* — the King has brought Ajax back!"

Ajax's mother moved forward and as she reached to the King's horse, he said,

"Your little boy had a fall on some rough stones. He has hurt his knee a little, but I do not think it is too serious."

"And you brought him back?" she replied in an awed voice.

"I think he has enjoyed the ride on my horse."

"It is very kind of Your Majesty," the woman said and reached up her arms to Ajax.

Before the King handed the little boy to her, he felt in his pocket and drew out a golden coin,

"Now you are to buy a present for your mother as well as one for yourself," he said to Ajax.

"Say thank you to His Majesty," cried his mother.

Holding the gold coin tightly in his hand, Ajax held up both his arms towards the King and with what Titania thought was just a slight hesitation, he bent down and kissed the boy on the cheek.

Then as he handed the small boy

into his mother's arms, the people around them began to clap their hands and cheer.

The spontaneous gesture was very moving and Titania could not prevent tears coming into her eyes.

She and the King turned their horses round and as they rode down the street the crowd followed them. They were still cheering when they reached the main road.

Only then, when they quickened their pace, could they leave the people behind them.

Titania felt quite certain that the story would be repeated all over the City and it would certainly be good for the King's reputation.

She did not say so aloud, but she thought by the way he looked at her and the faint smile on his lips, he understood what she was thinking.

They rode back to the Palace stables to find Darius and Kastri in an agitated state, because they did not know what had happened to them.

As they had been so far behind they had not seen the King picking up Ajax nor that instead of riding to the Palace they had detoured into the City.

"It was a shock, Your Majesty," said Darius, "when we arrived here to find no sign of you or Miss Brooke."

"We were not far away," the King informed him, "but we had a passenger with us, a small boy had hurt his knee and it was necessary to take him home."

"His mother and all the people in the street were very grateful," added Titania. "It was a very shabby and dingy street and the houses were all in a very bad state of repair."

"That goes for a good number of streets in the City," muttered Darius.

The King frowned.

"Why did no one tell me they were so bad?" he demanded. "They must be repaired. Surely the Government is aware of this situation."

"I think it is just a question of money, Your Majesty," replied Darius.

The King looked at Titania.

"I believe I have an answer to this problem. Make an appointment for me to see the Prime Minister and members of the Cabinet immediately after luncheon."

"I will do so, Sire," responded Darius.

Titania considered that she should now be getting back to her own room just in case Sophie sent for her.

"Thank you, Your Majesty, for a wonderful ride," she said to the King. "I know you have made a number of people very happy this morning, especially Ajax."

"And you have turned my eyes in a new direction. It will be interesting to know what comes of it."

"We can only hope it is gold,

Sire," Titania told him, "but I am sure you are quite prepared to accept other metals if, as I am told, they are nearly as valuable."

"Shall I quote your Nanny," asked the King, "and say that I will be very grateful for small mercies?"

Titania gave a little laugh and would have moved away, but the King said,

"I should have told you first thing this morning that a cable came through last night to say that your Nanny and Mercury left Tilbury yesterday."

"How wonderful!" cried Titania, "I cannot wait for you to see Mercury."

"I shall feel very humiliated if he puts my own horses to shame."

"He will not do that, but it will be marvellous for me to have him, and thank you, thank you."

She looked up at the King as she spoke and their eyes met.

And then she found it was very hard to look away.

Only when she was back in her own room, did Titania think it had been a very strange morning, not because of what had happened over Ajax or the King's reaction to her suggestion about the mountains.

It was because he had begun by being so cold, distant and reserved and she felt he had somehow withdrawn himself from her and they were no longer friends. Yet just now, when they were talking about Mercury and Nanny, he had been the same as when they had first met.

'However much I have upset him, he has now forgiven me,' Titania told herself and wanted to sing and dance because she was so glad.

Sophie sent for her an hour later and was most disagreeable because the string of pearls she was wearing yesterday had broken when she was being received by the dignitaries of a Northern town.

It was not Titania's fault, but Sophie complained she was badly looked after, no one bothered about her appearance and everything she wore needed attention.

It was all very unfair, but from long experience of her cousin's behaviour Titania knew not to answer back and so she merely accepted the abuse that was being hurled at her, although at the same time it made her more frightened than ever.

If Sophie ever heard that she had been out riding with the King, anything might happen and she was sure that the story of the King taking Ajax home would be repeated and re-repeated over the City before nightfall.

Undoubtedly someone would tell Prince Frederick about it adding that the King had been accompanied by a young woman. This would immediately, Titania reasoned, point a finger at her.

She wondered what she should do if Sophie forbade her ever to ride with the King again and in addition she would be extremely angry when she learned that Nanny and Mercury were on their way to the Palace.

Yet Sophie could hardly send them back although she could make considerable trouble for Nanny.

There was nothing Titania could do to prevent all this from happening and it made her increasingly apprehensive.

Later in the afternoon when Sophie had gone out, Titania found it impossible to sit down as she had intended and read the books she had brought from the library.

She moved restlessly around her boudoir.

Suddenly it occurred to her that there should be one or more books in the library about gold deposits and these would certainly be of interest to the King.

She remembered one particular book that her father had owned on that subject and wondered if she could find it. She was sure the King would never have read this book, which meant she might have some difficulty in finding what she wanted.

'If I go and look now,' she decided, 'I will have it ready when we can talk about the subject.'

She left her room and so that no one would notice her she went the rather unusual way to the library that Darius had showed her.

She entered through the door that opened behind the King's writing desk, thinking with satisfaction that she had seen no one on her way to the library.

She climbed up the steps onto the balcony and started to search amongst the older books for anything that looked as if it might contain information about prospecting for gold.

She found one book which she thought might prove interesting, but it was, however, very old, having been published over a century ago and she did not think it would be particularly helpful.

At least it was an encouraging start, but she searched further to no avail.

Then she had an idea that there might be a shelf on the other side of the library almost opposite the King's writing desk and this time she was lucky.

She found a book which she was certain the King would find most interesting as it described where rich deposits had been found in a number of countries and what type of geology was usually the most productive.

She put the book down on the floor of the balcony and looked to see if there were any more of a similar nature.

As she did so she heard voices.

Quickly, because she did not want to be seen, she crouched down on the floor of the balcony.

She expected it would be a servant or an *aide-de-camp* entering the library as it was certainly too soon for the King to have returned from the City.

Then, as she peeped through the gold leaves of the balustrade, she saw the door she had come through open.

To her surprise Prince Frederick came in followed by the two *aides-de-camp* who always accompanied him.

Titania had met them both and she had thought them rather like their Master, very pleased with themselves and not interested in anyone else.

Prince Frederick looked round to make sure there was no one in the library.

Then he said in a rather lower voice than he usually used,

"You see how easy it will be if you come in through this door. The King will have his back to you and will of course be reading or writing his book."

There was a scornful note in his voice over the last words which made Titania feel angry.

"Suppose he hears us?" one of the *aides-de-camp* asked the Prince.

He was a man called Henry and Titania particularly disliked him.

"He will hear nothing," asserted Prince Frederick firmly. "The stiletto will pierce his back and if it is driven in hard enough he will die immediately. Which of you is going to do it?"

He looked at his other *aide-de-camp*, who turned his head away from him.

"I cannot — do it — Your Royal Highness," he said in a voice which trembled.

"It is not like you to be chicken-hearted and I promise you both superior positions at Court once I am King."

Neither of the *aides-de-camp* spoke and he continued,

"You know as well as I do that his change of attitude in bringing those craftsmen from an obscure village into the City and carrying an injured child on his horse is making the people aware of him as they have never been before."

Prince Frederick paused for a moment as if he thought the *aides-de-camp* might say something.

Then as they both remained silent, he went on,

"I thought, as you are well aware, that if he remained a recluse for long enough, the people would cry out that I should take his place and he would be forced to abdicate. What is now happening is upsetting all my plans."

"I know, Your Royal Highness, it is extremely difficult," Henry spoke up at last, "but perhaps, if we remove the girl, he would revert to his normal behaviour, which would make matters better for you."

"I will deal with her later," snarled Prince Frederick. "She can have an unfortunate accident. Fall out of a window or drown in the lake. *She is no problem.*"

"But once she is no longer around," persisted Henry, "it might mean that the King will return to his isolation."

"It is too late," snapped Prince Frederick. "I have waited long enough. I intend to be King and nothing will stop me."

He looked first at one of the *aides-de-camp* and then at the other.

"Very well, as I cannot allow you to mess things up, I will kill him myself. All we have to do is to open the window which is here just behind his chair, which will show how the assassins entered and killed the

King while he was working on his book."

"Your Royal Highness is very clever," said Henry and the other *aide-de-camp* murmured the same sentiment.

"Now it is all settled," announced Prince Frederick with satisfaction, "and we will do it tonight as soon as it is dark. With any luck no one will think of disturbing the King until the early hours of the morning when they have been told to escort him up to bed."

He looked round the library again.

Titania turned her head away in case, by some terrible mischance, he would see her eyes looking at him through the golden leaves.

Then Prince Frederick looked again towards the writing table.

There was an unpleasant smile on his lips as if he could already see his half-brother lying dead and know that he was the King of Velidos.

He turned round sharply and walked from the library with the two *aides-de-camp* following him, closing the door behind them.

Titania could hardly believe what she had heard.

She was trembling with the sheer horror of it.

She was so terrified that she found it impossible to move for a long time after Prince Frederick and his entourage had left.

Could it really be possible that he

intended to kill the King himself? And that she also would die in some mysterious way from his hand?

It was a treacherous and wicked plot and she realised that the only person who could prevent it happening was herself.

Now it was vitally important that no one should see her leaving the library as by some mischance they might mention it to Prince Frederick, as if he suspected she had overheard what he was plotting, he would undoubtedly kill her immediately.

There was only one way she could prevent it from happening and that was that she must stay where she was until the King returned.

Every minute she waited for him seemed like an hour.

She began to be afraid that Prince Frederick had changed his plan and had killed the King in some other way before he returned to the Palace. She knew, even as she thought about it, that it was just her imagination.

She had to keep calm and sensible if she was to save the King.

At last, when it was nearly five o'clock, the main door to the library opened and the King entered followed by a servant who was asking him if he required any tea.

"No thank you," he answered, "but I would like a glass of champagne later in the evening. See that you put a bottle on ice."

"I will do so at once, Your Majesty."

The servant bowed and left the room.

The King walked towards his desk and it was then that Titania rose to her feet and started to climb down the steps onto the floor.

The King looked at her in surprise.

"I did not know you were here, Titania. I suppose you have been finding yourself another book to read."

Titania ran across the floor towards him.

When she reached him, for a moment the words would not come to her lips.

She could only look at him and

he saw that she was trembling.

"What on earth has happened?" he asked. "What is the matter and why are you so upset?"

Titania put out her hand to hold on to him and in a whisper, which did not sound like her own voice, she told him,

"Prince Frederick is going to — murder you and — I too am — going to — die!"

The words came out incoherently and the King stared at her as if he could not believe what he had heard.

Then as he realised how genuinely upset she was, he said calmly,

"Come and sit down and tell me what has happened."

He drew Titania towards the sofa

by the fireplace and she sat down obediently.

At the same time she hung on to his hand with both of hers, as if she was afraid that should she let him go she might lose him.

"Now tell me what has happened," repeated the King.

Slowly, finding every word difficult to utter and trembling as she did so, Titania told him what she had overheard.

She explained why she had come to the library to look for a book about prospecting for gold, how she had heard voices and thought it was the servants and, because she was in the library without permission, she had crouched down on the floor of the balcony.

Then she began to relate how Prince Frederick had entered the room and tried to remember every word he had said and every reply that had come from his *aides-de-camp*.

The King did not speak or interrupt.

His fingers merely tightened on Titania's and his eyes were on her face.

Finally, when she had described how the Prince had gone away with a last look round at the library, she cried frantically,

"You must save yourself — you must have him arrested immediately. Oh, please — please believe what — I have told you."

"I do believe you," answered the

King quietly. "Now I want you to be very brave and sensible and go to your room and stay there."

"But he may — come and — kill me as he — has said he will."

"You will be protected, although no one will be aware of it," replied the King. "I want you to lock your door and tell anyone who is interested that you feel unwell and have gone to bed and do not want to be disturbed."

"What — will — you do?"

"Thanks to you," said the King emphatically, "I will live to see another day."

He took her hand which was still holding onto his and raised it to his lips.

"Thank you, Titania. Now you

must leave me at once, because I have so much to do."

"Promise — me you will — be very careful," begged Titania.

"I promise you."

"You must let me know — later tonight as soon as anything has happened. You know I will be unable to — sleep and will be praying frantically that — you will not be — hurt."

"That is what I want you to do and to believe that good will triumph over evil as it always has."

He rose to his feet and then he thought for a moment.

"It would be a mistake for anyone to see you leaving the library who might inadvertently tell Prince Frederick you were here when he came in to plot my murder."

"That is why I — stayed here until — you came back."

"That was very brave of you," the King told her, "and are you brave enough to return the way you came which Darius showed you?"

"Yes, Sire, of course."

"Then lock yourself in and re-member that no one except your maid will be allowed to come near you."

He took her to the door through which Prince Frederick had entered the library and he was aware that she shivered as they passed through it.

He escorted her to the door which led into the garden.

"Go to your room quickly," he

said. "Do not linger anywhere and start praying because we both need it."

Titania looked up at him.

She thought, as this morning, that when their eyes met there was a strange expression in his.

She turned away and hurried through the garden. She was almost certain there was no one there to see her.

The King turned back into the library.

He rang the bell which summoned not the servants but his two *aides-de-camp* when he needed them and Darius and Kastri came at once to see what he required.

When they had closed the door he informed them of everything that Titania had told him and gave them their orders.

Horrified, but obeying him exactly as he knew they would, they hurried away.

After the King had dined alone as he always did and the servants had left the dining room, Darius and Kastri joined him.

"You have everything ready?" the King asked them.

"Everything, Sire," replied Darius.

The King walked into the library and extinguished all the lights except one on his desk.

He had recently installed electric light in the Palace which the people had thought was sensational.

Darius and Kastri now carried

something large and heavy into the library and set it down on the chair in front of the King's writing desk.

It was an hour later that Prince Frederick and his two *aides-de-camp* crept in from the garden, wearing soft-soled shoes which made no sound.

They entered the King's dining room and moving across it very slowly opened the door into the library.

Ahead Prince Frederick could see his half-brother quite clearly seated at his desk crouched over the book he was writing.

There was an expression of grim triumph on his face as he moved stealthily forward.

Raising his arm he brought the long, thin deadly stiletto which he held in his right hand down with all his strength into the King's back.

Even as he did so and before he could release his hold of the stiletto, the lights in the library flashed on.

The curtains over the long windows opened and into the room stepped the King, the Prime Minister, the Lord Chamberlain and the Lord Chief Justice.

Standing on the balcony were Darius and Kastri with revolvers in their hands.

Prince Frederick stared at them.

Then he looked down at the dummy figure into which he had just stuck his stiletto. It was very lifelike, but with no face, only a false wig to imitate the King's hair.

For a moment there was complete silence.

Then the King said,

"I deeply regret that this should have occurred, Frederick, and that you were so anxious to take my place that you were prepared to murder me."

"I can explain," answered Prince Frederick quickly. "It was just a joke."

The King did not deign to answer, but merely continued,

"You know as well as I do that the punishment for those guilty of treason against the person of the King is to be beheaded."

One of the Prince's *aides-de-*

camp let out a scream of terror and flung himself onto the floor.

"We were made to do it, we were made to do it!" he cried.

The King took no notice of him.

"I have decided, however," he continued, still looking at Prince Frederick, "that as you are my half-brother, there should be no scandal attached to those who bear our name, so I intend to be extremely merciful."

"I can explain —" Prince Frederick began to say again, but the King held up his hand for silence.

"I do not wish for any explanation, nor do I want a trial. What I have decided is that you and your wife will go immediately into exile. You will leave early tomorrow for the Island of Platicos where you will stay for the rest of your life. You can have anything you require and you and your wife will be quite comfortable."

He paused for a moment.

"At the same time should you attempt to leave Platicos or ever again set foot on Velidos soil, you will be taken in front of the Lord Chief Justice who will administer the Law of the Land as it is written for those who commit treason against the King."

Prince Frederick was defeated and he knew it.

He turned and without a word walked out of the library followed by his *aides-de-camp* who were both in tears.

CHAPTER SEVEN

When Titania reached her bedroom after leaving the King to his preparations to foil Prince Frederick's plot, she went down on her knees beside the bed.

She prayed more fervently than she ever had prayed in her whole life that the King would be saved.

She thought nothing could be more terrible than to learn tomorrow or perhaps tonight, that things had gone wrong and he was dead.

She wondered, if that happened,

whether she would be brave enough to tell the truth, but there would perhaps be no point if he was no longer alive.

'Save him, God — please save — him,' she prayed over and over again.

Then as she prayed, she knew that she loved the King.

She had not realised it before, because she knew so little about love.

It had been a joy and a delight to be with him and she had been miserable when he had stayed away and did not come riding in the early morning with her.

Now she understood that she had given him her heart.

She loved him to the point that if

he died she had no wish to go on living.

'I love him, God,' she prayed, 'please — save him — please — *please.*'

She felt as if she was sending a thousand prayers up to Heaven on wings and somehow they would reach God.

Equally she recognised that the whole situation was desperately dangerous, not only for the King, but for herself.

'I do not matter,' she said beneath her breath. 'If I die no one will worry, but if he dies then — everything that might benefit this country will be left undone. The whole population will miss him even if they are not aware of it.'

She prayed until she heard the maids come in to bring her bath as they always did before dinner.

It was with the greatest difficulty that she behaved naturally, talking to the maids in their language. She hoped she looked calm and not agitated, as far as they were concerned.

Tonight she told them that she had a headache and would not be going down to dinner and would they please arrange for her to have a light meal in her room.

They were very solicitous that she should be feeling unwell and because she thought she must keep up the pretence, she climbed into bed having had her bath.

She lay back against the pillows.

"I hope you're not sickening for something, miss," one of the maids said. "There be very bad fevers around here sometimes and they make one feel awful."

"I will be alright," replied Titania. "It is just that I am overtired."

"It's all that riding you does," the maid answered.

Then she went on,

"I hear His Majesty brought a little boy who had been hurt back to his mother when he'd been riding this morning."

"Who told you that?" asked Titania.

"Oh, they're all talking about it downstairs and everyone in the City is astonished at the King's kindness."

Titania could not help smiling as this was what she was hoping they would be saying about the King.

She was only apprehensive that Sophie would hear that she had been riding with him as, of course, the maids who looked after her were well aware of her early morning excursions.

When they called her she had already left her room and when she returned, she had changed from her riding clothes. She had made them promise not to tell anyone else that she went riding early in the morning.

She wondered now if it was something she would ever do again.

She could not imagine what would happen to Sophie when the

King denounced Prince Frederick and she did not want to think about the penalty in Velidos for treason.

She knew in London it had meant all down the ages that the offender was taken to the Tower and beheaded.

It was impossible for Titania to eat any of the delicious dishes that were brought upstairs for her dinner as she was too agitated.

When her tray was taken away, she told the maids that she did not wish to be disturbed as she was going to sleep and they hoped that she would have a restful night.

At last she was alone.

It was agony not to know what was happening downstairs and what the King was doing.

Again she feared that at the last moment something might go wrong and he would die.

'I love him — *I love him,*' Titania prayed. 'Please — *save him.*'

Much later, in fact it must have been nearly midnight, Titania was still awake and praying, when she heard a knock on the communicating door that opened into her boudoir.

She jumped out of bed and pulling on her dressing gown she ran to the door.

It was Darius.

"What — has — happened?" she asked breathlessly.

"Everything is all right," replied Darius. "You have saved His Majesty's life."

Titania took a deep breath and it was with the greatest difficulty that she did not burst into tears from sheer relief.

"Thanks to you, His Majesty was prepared and when Prince Frederick came into the library there were witnesses of what he was attempting to do waiting behind the curtains."

He told Titania about the dummy and who the witnesses were and how he and Kastri were stationed on the balcony.

"His Royal Highness has been very mercifully treated," he finished. "His Majesty has sent him and the Princess into exile on Platicos which is a pretty island and boasts a small Palace, which was built by His Majesty's grandfather when he wanted to take a holiday."

"And they have to — stay there?" asked Titania hesitatingly

"They are forbidden to leave the island, but otherwise they can have everything they may require."

The relief was so overwhelming that Titania felt as if she might sink onto the floor.

"I must leave you now," Darius informed her, "but His Majesty wanted you to know at once what had happened and also that it will be impossible for him to go riding tomorrow morning."

"Of course, I can quite understand."

"You have been very wonderful

and everyone who knows what has occurred is in your debt and extremely grateful to you."

To Titania's surprise he went down on one knee and, taking her hand in his, kissed it.

Without another word he turned, walked across the boudoir and left her.

Titania climbed back to bed.

Now she prayed again, but it was a prayer of thankfulness that God had heard her fervent pleading.

The King was safe.

Titania awoke and realised that it was very late in the morning.

She had not gone to sleep for a long time after Darius had left her and even now she felt a little drowsy.

At the same time, when she re-membered that the King was safe, she felt as if a shaft of sunlight was sweeping through her body.

'I must get up,' she determined, 'and I wonder when I can see him.'

It was a question she asked herself every minute that passed and she wanted to be quite certain that he was alive and really had survived the dastardly plot against him.

'He is so kind and so wonderful and there is so much for him to do now that he is interested in his people and in making Velidos prosperous.'

She remembered that she had left the book on prospecting for gold, which she wanted the King to read, on the balcony in the library.

It would still be lying on the spot where she had hidden it from Prince Frederick and she thought that when the King sent for her she would tell him about it.

She ate her breakfast alone and did not like to leave the boudoir or her bedroom until she was told she could do so.

She supposed that her cousin would be packing up to leave on the ship that was to take her and Prince Frederick to Platicos and she did not expect that Sophie would want or be allowed to say goodbye to her.

It must have been nearly half-past nine when there was a knock on her bedroom door.

Titania crossed the room to open it.

Outside was the lady's maid who spoke English and who had been attending Princess Sophie.

"What is it, Christa?" asked Titania.

"Her Royal Highness," replied Christa, "says that you are to go with her to Platicos. You are to hurry and have your clothes packed. Their Royal Highnesses are leaving in two hours."

Titania stared at the woman.

"Did you — say I was to go — with the Princess?"

"That is what she says, miss."

Titania pushed her to one side and ran down the passage.

She ran without thinking or considering anything but the horror she felt. The idea of having to go into exile with Sophie and Prince Frederick was terrifying.

She ran through the hall and along the corridor which led into the library.

She pulled open the door and rushed in.

The King was at the far end of the room, not sitting at his writing table, but standing in front of the window.

He heard her approach and turned round.

As Titania ran towards him he saw the expression of horror on her face and the fear in her eyes.

"What is the matter, what has happened?"

Titania flung herself against him and had to hold on to him or she would have fallen down.

"They — tell me," she stammered in a breathless voice that was hardly articulate, "that I am to — go with Sophie into — exile. Please, please do not — make me — do so. Please — let me stay here."

The words seemed to fall out of her lips without Titania realising what she was saying.

The King put his arms around her.

"Do you think I could possibly lose you?" he asked.

Then his lips were on hers.

He kissed her, not gently but fiercely, as if it was something he had long wanted to do and could no longer control himself.

To Titania it was as if the Heavens had opened and a light from God suddenly enveloped her.

When she felt the urgent pressure of his lips, her body seemed to melt into his.

She gave him not only her heart but her soul.

The King kissed her until she felt as if they were no longer of this world, but were flying up into the sky.

Then he raised his head and looked down at her.

"I love you," he said and his voice was very deep.

"And I love you — I love you," murmured Titania, "and I would rather die than have to go away —

and never see you again."

"You will not die, my darling, but you will live to show me exactly how I can love my people as you want me to."

Titania hid her face against his shoulder.

"Did you — really say — you love me?" she whispered.

"I have loved you from the first moment I saw you, but I felt it was something I dared not feel, because everything I have ever cared for has always been taken from me."

Titania realised he was thinking of how he had lost his dog and how cruel his stepmother had been to him.

Without being aware of it she moved even closer to him and almost as if she was speaking to herself she told him,

"No one shall ever hurt you again."

"That is what I thought you might say to me," sighed the King, "but I was desperately afraid."

Titania looked up in surprise.

"Afraid of — what?"

"That I would not be allowed to marry you," the King replied.

Titania gave a little gasp.

Somehow the thought of marriage had never occurred to her when she was thinking about the King and loving him.

"But of course — not," she said. "I am sure you are — not allowed — to marry a — commoner."

"Do you think," the King asked

her, "that I would offer you anything else? Even a morganatic marriage. My darling, I love you too much for that."

Because of the emotion in his voice and the look in his eyes, Titania felt a quiver of rapture run through her.

She hid her face against him again.

"I — do not — understand," she whispered.

"I tried to steel myself against you and to tell myself that it was unlikely that you would love me and therefore I must ignore what I felt for you. But it was completely impossible."

"Is that why you — did not — come riding?" Titania questioned.

"It was, and then when I knew I could not lose you and had no wish to live without you, my prayers were answered."

"Your — prayers?"

"I prayed to every God you and I have ever talked about, and, naturally, as I am half Greek, I prayed to the Gods who lived on Olympus with the Goddess of Love amongst them."

His arms tightened round her and once again Titania felt rapture moving through her body.

The King continued,

"As if it was a voice from Heaven, I was told what to do."

"What — was — that?"

"I cabled my Ambassador in London and told him to send me your mother's family tree."

Titania stared at him in astonishment.

"But why?" she asked. "And what has — it to do with — *us*?"

"I was not really sure, but it was what I was told to do by a Power greater than myself."

With his arms around Titania he drew her a little nearer to his desk.

"This is what arrived this morning," he said, "and it has just been decoded."

He handed Titania a piece of paper and she looked at it in surprise.

Then she read,

"In answer to Your Majesty's request, the father of Lady Rupert Brooke was the Chieftain of the

McHelms, an ancient clan dating back to the Picts. His wife was Isa Falkner, a direct descendant of Robert the Bruce, King of Scotland from 1306 to 1329.

I trust that this is the information Your Majesty required.

I remain, Your Majesty's most humble and obedient servant."

It was signed with the signature of the Ambassador and Titania stared at the paper before saying,

"I knew that Mama was related to Robert the Bruce, but the English have never thought very much of him, because he drove them out of Scotland before he came to the throne."

"Whatever the English thought or did not think, a King is always a

King. That is why, my precious one, *we can be married.* You will be my Queen and help me to make Velidos exactly the Kingdom you and I want it to be."

Titania threw her arms round him.

"I do not believe it. I am dreaming. I never thought for one moment that even though I love you — we could be — married."

"We are going to be married immediately," insisted the King, "because I do not want to be without you for one minute more than necessary. Also there is sure to be a great deal of gossip already about my disreputable half-brother going to Platicos. So we must give our people something else to talk about and what could be better than a Royal Wedding?"

"They have — already had — one," murmured Titania.

"Ours will be very different and it will be you, my darling, who will make it different. They will have something to remember for the rest of their lives."

She pulled the King's head down towards hers.

"That is just the sort of thing I want you to say. You are so wonderful and I want your people to know it and to — love you — as I do."

"As long as you love me, nothing else matters."

"I love you with all of — me," answered Titania, "my heart, my soul are — all yours. Are you quite,

quite sure that — nothing can prevent us — from being together?"

"I am quite, quite sure," the King smiled at her tenderly. "And, my darling, because you want our people to be happy, we will do everything in our power to make them as happy as we are."

Titania thought as she looked up at him that she had never seen a man look so happy.

There was an expression in the King's eyes that made her as thrilled as if the sunshine was burning inside her breasts.

As if he knew what she was feeling, he pulled her closer.

He kissed her until it was impossible for her to think of anything else except the wonder of his kisses.

It must have been an hour later when the King said,

"Frederick's ship will have left by now and I am going to announce my engagement to you and that we are to be married in four days time."

He looked at Titania as he spoke as if he feared she might object and say it was too soon.

Because she knew what he was thinking, she merely replied,

"Must we wait — so long?"

The King laughed.

"I adore you," he told her, "and you always say the unexpected. Apart from anything else, my precious, I want to explore you and everything about you, just as I have already given orders that the most experienced metal prospectors in the world are to be asked to come to Velidos and explore our mountains."

"That is marvellous," cried Titania. "I know that because God is so good to us we will find something fantastically valuable and everyone in the country will benefit."

"Apart from anything else they will richly benefit just because you are their Queen," added the King.

Then he was kissing her again.

To Titania it was a challenge that the King had decided they should be married in four days time as it gave her very little time to plan what should be done.

He told her that he was already considering that there should be fireworks for the people and a merry-go-round and amusements for the children, which they would never have experienced.

When she learnt that he had already given the orders, Titania flung her arms round him saying,

"You are wonderful, wonderful, exactly the King I want you to be."

"I think of what you would want," he said, "and then I know it is the right thing to do."

They walked round the Palace hand in hand with all the Courtiers and servants smiling benignly at them.

Titania thought she was living in a paradise that she could never have even imagined.

As the King was planning ways to delight his people, Titania thought quickly that she too must make her wedding different in every way from Sophie's.

She turned to Darius.

"How many towns are there in Velidos?"

He thought for a moment and then answered,

"I think there are eight what you might call towns and the rest are only little villages."

"Then I tell you what you will have to arrange immediately —"

Darius was listening and she explained,

"I want each town to send a little girl of six or seven years old to be one of my bridesmaids. There will be two from the City and that will make ten altogether. They can wear white dresses, which their mothers can make for them very easily out of cheap muslin, and we at the Palace must provide wreaths for their heads and small bouquets for them to carry."

"That is a brilliant idea!" exclaimed Darius. "And it will please everyone."

"That is what I thought," continued Titania, "and I suggest that the King makes an order that a boy of sixteen is chosen from each town and again two from here in the City, who will wear the national costume and escort him as a bodyguard, besides, of course, his soldiers."

Darius was delighted with the idea and so was the King when he heard about it.

"I knew you would think of something different, my darling," he said to Titania.

It was impossible for her to reply because he was kissing her.

For her own wedding dress she had the inspiration of sending for the woman in the little village who made lace so beautifully and found that she had already moved into one of the empty shops in the City's main street.

Titania had brought a white dress which Nanny had insisted on her buying before she came away and when a train was added to it and the lace decorated it, it looked gloriously beautiful.

Almost like a fairy tale wedding gown.

The King sent for the Crown Jewels, which had not seen the light of day since his mother had worn them. They were different from those that had been specially made for his stepmother.

"These," he said harshly, "are to be sold and the money spent in building a hospital in the City."

His mother's jewels were of Greek design and stunningly exquisite.

Titania put on the Crown and the magnificent diamond necklace and she knew by the expression in the King's eyes how lovely she must look.

She had not forgotten what she had been told his stepmother had done. As well as the Crown Jewels having been stored away, so had a great many other objects which had adorned the Palace.

As Darius had said, it was an Aladdin's Cave and when she and the King inspected the rooms filled with what his stepmother had discarded, they could hardly believe their eyes.

There were exquisite examples of Dresden and Sevres china and gold goblets embellished with precious stones.

There were chandeliers that the German Queen had thought too extravagant because they held so many candles.

There were collections of jewel-inlaid snuff boxes and also to the King's delight a number of pictures by famous artists. His stepmother had thought they overloaded the walls.

He gave orders that everything was to be brought out and cleaned and placed in the rooms where they must have been in the past. Some of the older servants remembered exactly where each object belonged.

When Titania saw the transformation of the dull reception rooms, she clapped her hands with delight.

"Now it looks like the sort of Palace you should be living in," she said to the King.

"I want it to be a Palace for you," he answered, "and, my darling, I think we should travel a little to add to our collection."

"I would love that," she said simply. "I am so happy because wherever we are together is like being in Heaven."

"That is exactly what I was thinking," he sighed.

Despite the rush their wedding plans were all carried out to perfection.

And to add to Titania's happiness Darius came to tell her that Nanny and Mercury were due to arrive in Velidos the day before the Royal Wedding.

"My life is now complete," she cried, as she thanked Darius with tears in her eyes.

When Titania left the Palace with

the Lord Chamberlain there were many more spectators in the streets than there had been for Sophie's wedding.

She drove in the State glass carriage to the Cathedral.

The cheers of the crowd were spontaneously enthusiastic and everyone who looked at her seemed to be smiling.

Her bridesmaids were waiting at the foot of the Cathedral steps and they looked like a bunch of flowers with their white dresses and their wreaths and bouquets.

The ten pretty little girls were very excited, as were their parents.

Titania spoke to each one of them and then as they followed her up the steps to the West door, the crowd cheered and shouted, realising what a beautiful picture they made.

"Good luck and long life."

The Cathedral was packed and many were standing at the back unable to find a seat, but Titania had made certain that Nanny was given a seat right at the front.

A fanfare of trumpets greeted Titania as she entered and she could see the King waiting for her at the end of the aisle. It was with the greatest difficulty that she did not run towards him.

The young men in their national costume made a spectacular bodyguard on either side of the aisle.

When Titania reached the King it was impossible not to put out her hand and slip it into his.

His fingers tightened on hers.

Then as the Archbishop began the service, Titania was certain that the angels were singing overhead and God was blessing their marriage as He had brought them together when they had prayed to Him.

As the King crowned her, Titania prayed that she would deserve the faith of him and his people.

When the service was over, the King with Titania on his arm walked slowly down the aisle and the young men in their national costume followed the small bridesmaids.

As they stepped out through the West door, they made such a

colourful picture that the crowds below almost went mad with excitement.

They had all brought flower petals to throw at the bride and bridegroom and now there was no doubt that their enthusiasm came from their hearts.

Holding tightly on to the King with one hand, Titania waved with the other.

She realised that this was really the beginning of his reign and she was determined that it would be a reign that would be remembered and respected in the centuries ahead.

Following the King's instructions a whole playground had been arranged for the children. There were not only merry-go-rounds, but Punch and Judy shows and dozens of other attractions which would continue until nightfall.

The fireworks entranced the whole City and there were no citizens of any age who did not find a wine or fruit cup in which to drink the health and happiness of the bride and bridegroom.

A crowd gathered at the foot of the Palace steps and they cheered and shouted until the King and Queen came out.

It was, of course, Titania who suggested that they walked down the steps to the crowd who were being kept back from climbing up to them by the soldiers who were on guard.

Then when he and Titania were only a few steps above the people, he made a short speech, thanking them for coming to his wedding and joining in his happiness.

He told them that from this moment, because he now had his beautiful Queen beside him, they were starting a new reign and he hoped it would make everyone in Velidos happy and prosperous.

"I need your help," announced the King. "As you well know, there are many houses which need repairing and paint to make them look more attractive. We want to attract tourists to this country who will help to bring us the prosperity we all need."

There were cheers as the crowd

understood what he was saying.

"I want every man amongst you, who is not engaged on other important work to make the City look a model which other countries will envy."

There was a murmur of approval as he continued,

"I want every woman who is clever with her hands, as I know most of you are, to make articles which we can sell. I am sure that in a few months tourists from all over Europe will be anxious to see what we are doing and come to visit Velidos."

Now the crowd was listening to him intently.

"We will have to provide hotels and other accommodation, which I intend to start building immediately. But as I say, I can only achieve this if every man and woman who belongs to this land helps me with their crafts and with their belief in what we are attempting to achieve."

Titania noticed that there were several men who she was sure were newspaper reporters taking down every word the King was saying in his speech.

As he finished there was wild applause and shouts from the people of what they could do and how they would help.

"I am so proud of you, Alexius, my husband and my King," Titania whispered into his ear. "You have given hope and inspiration to your people and I know that they will do everything in their power to make your dream for them come true."

It was some time before the bride and bridegroom were able to return to the Palace.

When they did get inside, the King, without saying goodnight to anyone, drew Titania up the stairs.

"We have done our duty," he told her. "Now I want you to myself."

He took her along the passage not to her bedroom, but to the one that was part of the Master Suite.

She knew it had always been used by the Queens of Velidos and when they entered there was no lady's maid or valet waiting for them.

The King closed the door.

"Now at last, my darling, I have you alone, as I have been waiting for you ever since early this morning."

"It was such a lovely wedding," sighed Titania.

"And you were the most beautiful bride any man could ever imagine."

Very gently he took the tiara which had replaced the Crown from her head and undid the diamond and pearl necklace she wore round her neck.

She thought that he would kiss her, but instead he undid the back of her gown.

Then he said,

"Get into bed, my precious darling, while I get rid of my finery. I will only be a few minutes."

He went into his own room and Titania did as he told her.

She threw her wedding gown over a chair and then she put on a very pretty nightgown which was lying waiting for her on the bed.

As she lay back against the pillows she thought it was impossible to be happier or more grateful to God for giving her such a wonderful husband.

Titania could imagine all too easily what sort of man her uncle would have chosen for her.

It did not seem possible after the years of being treated as if she was just an encumbrance that she was now the Queen of such a lovely country.

The door opened and the King

entered.

He did not come straight to her as she expected and instead he drew back the curtains.

Outside there was a full moon in the sky and the stars were shining brightly.

He stood for a moment looking up as if he was speaking to God and then he turned round and came towards Titania.

She had left only one small light burning by the side of the bed.

She had no idea how beautiful she looked with her fair hair falling over her shoulders with her grey eyes shining with the love she felt for the King.

He climbed into the bed and pulled her into his arms.

Then as she nestled against him, he said,

"Can this really be happening? After all that has happened to me in my life, I can hardly believe that you are really mine and that some-one will not snatch you away from me."

"I am yours now and for ever," Titania told him, "and no one will ever hurt you again, my wonderful husband. I will always look after you and protect you."

The King drew her a little closer.

"As I shall protect you," he said and his voice was very deep. "I love you, my darling, you will be my whole life and I can see and think of nothing but you."

"I am afraid that you are going to

have to think of a great many other matters as well," Titania said softly. "But please let us do everything together, it will be fun and nothing will be too difficult for us."

"I love you, I adore you," murmured the King and his lips met hers.

He kissed her at first gently as if she was infinitely precious.

Then as he felt the ecstasy and rapture moving through her, his kisses became more passionate and more possessive.

To Titania it was as if they were climbing up the mountains together and together they touched the snowy peaks at the top of them.

She could not believe anyone could feel such joy without dying at the wonder of it.

This was love.

This was what she had sought and thought she would never be able to find, just as the King had tried to throw away his heart because he was afraid of being hurt over and over again.

She clasped her arms around his neck.

"I love you — I love you," she tried to say against his lips.

"I adore and worship you, my glorious Titania and my heart, which you have given me back, is yours from now to Eternity."

Then as he made her his, Titania touched the stars.

They both entered into a Heaven that was waiting just for them.

It was filled with love.

The Love which all mankind longs for and seeks and which only some are fortunate enough to find.

It is the Love of God which is Eternal.

THE LATE DAME
BARBARA CARTLAND

Barbara Cartland who sadly died in May 2000 at the age of nearly 99 was the world's most famous romantic novelist who wrote 723 books in her lifetime with worldwide sales of over 1 billion copies and her books were translated into 36 different languages.

As well as romantic novels, she wrote historical biographies, 6 autobiographies, theatrical plays, books of advice on life, love, vitamins and cookery. She also found time to be a political speaker and television and radio personality.

She wrote her first book at the age of 21 and this was called *Jigsaw*. It became an immediate bestseller and sold 100,000 copies in hardback and was translated into 6 different languages. She wrote continuously throughout her life, writing bestsellers for an astonishing 76 years. Her books have always been immensely popular in the United States, where in 1976 her current books were at numbers 1 & 2 in the B. Dalton bestsellers list, a feat never achieved before or since by any author.

Barbara Cartland became a legend in her own lifetime and will be best remembered for her wonderful romantic novels, so loved by her millions of readers throughout the world.

Her books will always be treasured for their moral message, her pure and innocent heroines, her good looking and dashing heroes and above all her belief that the power of love is more important than anything else in everyone's life.

The employees of Thorndike Press hope you have enjoyed this Large Print book. All our Thorndike, Wheeler, and Kennebec Large Print titles are designed for easy reading, and all our books are made to last. Other Thorndike Press Large Print books are available at your library, through selected bookstores, or directly from us.

For information about titles, please call:
(800) 223-1244

or visit our website at:
gale.com/thorndike

To share your comments, please write:
Publisher
Thorndike Press
10 Water St., Suite 310
Waterville, ME 04901